Food of the Dogs
a golden retriever mystery

Neil S. Plakcy

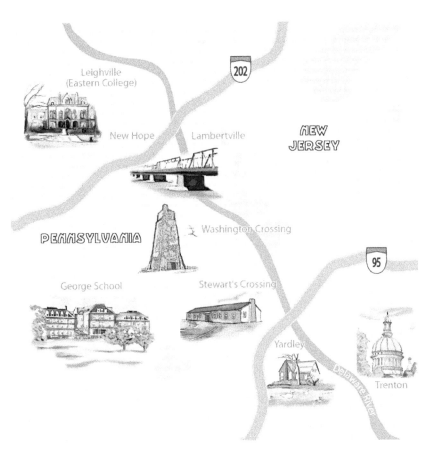

Copyright 2024 Neil S. Plakcy

This cozy mystery is a work of fiction. Names, characters, places, and incidents either are products of the author's imagination or are used fictitiously. Any resemblance to actual events or locales or persons, living or dead, is entirely coincidental. All rights reserved, including the right of reproduction in whole or in part in any form.

NO AI TRAINING: Without in any way limiting the author's [and publisher's] exclusive rights under copyright, any use of this publication to "train" generative artificial intelligence (AI) technologies to generate text is expressly prohibited. The author reserves all rights to license uses of this work for generative AI training and development of machine learning language models.

Reviews

Mr. Plakcy did a terrific job in this cozy mystery. He has a smooth writing style that kept the story flowing evenly. The dialogue and descriptions were right on target.

Red Adept

Steve and Rochester become quite a team and Neil Plakcy is the kind of writer that I want to tell me this story. It's a fun read which will keep you turning pages very quickly.

Amos Lassen – *Amazon top 100 reviewer Amos Lassen*

In Dog We Trust is a very well-crafted mystery that kept me guessing up until Steve figured out where things were going.

E-book addict reviews

Neil Plakcy's *Kingdom of Dog* is supposed to be about the former computer hacker, now college professor, Steve Levitan, but it is his golden retriever Rochester who is the real amateur sleuth in this delightful academic mystery. This is no talking dog book, though. Rochester doesn't need anything more than his wagging tail and doggy smile to win over readers and help solve crimes. I absolutely fell in love with this brilliant dog who digs up clues and points the silly humans towards the evidence.

– Christine Kling, author of *Circle of Bones*.

Author's Note: Time

Readers sometimes get confused about the timeline of the books, and I understand—I do, too! But I want to keep things realistic, so Rochester can't age too quickly. The first book in the series, *In Dog We Trust*, was written in real time as I was writing it, so it takes place in the fall of 2010. Rochester was a year-old rescue then.

The next books follow a few months apart, so by now we are in the fall of 2014, and Rochester is a sprightly five years old. It's my goal to continue writing books set a few months apart. That gives me a lot more books to write before Rochester becomes a senior citizen.

Chapter 1
Famous Last Words

"I now pronounce you husband and wife," Rabbi Rob announced, the audience applauded, and Rochester, our golden retriever, barked as Lili and I shared our first kiss as a married couple. Rochester had to get in on it, of course, going up on his hind legs and trying to nose his way between us. The audience laughed, and both of us reached down to stroke his soft fur.

Rochester had been a champ at the ceremony, delivering the rings to me in a gold mesh pouch around his neck, though as Lili feared he had made several detours down the aisle to stop and sniff the guests.

The wedding reception was everything we hoped it would be. Friar Lake, the conference center I managed in the Pennsylvania countryside, looked beautiful in the early fall sunshine. The stone buildings glowed and the lawns and trees were verdant. It was wonderful to be able to expose our family and friends to the place where I spent my days.

The food was delicious, prepared by a Kosher caterer who had been one of Lili's students. We had a guest performance by the Rising Suns, the a cappella group from Eastern College, where Lili and I worked, and one of the singers was also our DJ. He played the right kind of music for dancing, yet we could still have conversations, which to me was the main point of a gathering of family and friends. For our first dance as a married couple, we'd asked him to play Starship's "Nothing's Gonna Stop Us Now," and it was wonderful to have people join us on the dance floor after the first chorus.

The liquor flowed freely, and Lili's exuberant Latin family mingled well with my more laid-back cousins and our Stewart's Crossing friends. Columbus Day weekend of 2014 marked a successful and happy progress in my relationship with Lili.

Then Lili's cousin Mimo got into an argument with his son Victor. Mimo was a broad-shouldered blustery guy who had the same wavy auburn hair as Lili, though his was tamed down with lots of hair gel. Victor was taller and slimmer than his father, his dark hair cut in a fade. Both radiated macho energy.

Lili and I were standing nearby when the shouting started. Most of it was in Spanish, so I had no idea what was going down. I turned to Lili. "What are they arguing about?"

She cocked an ear in that direction. "Oh, it's the same old story. Victor wants to be a poet, and Mimo wants him to be a lawyer. Preferably an immigration attorney, to help refugees."

"I spoke to Victor earlier. He said that he's in graduate school studying poetry but he knows he can't make a living at that, so he's planning to become a teacher. Isn't that good enough for his father?"

"You know fathers and sons," Lili said. "They're always going to argue."

I did know a fair bit about that, but I wasn't going to let their argument ruin my wedding. With Rochester by my side, I walked over to them and put one hand on each man's shoulder. "Mimo, Victor. Can we lower the volume on this discussion?"

"When my father wants to make a point, he can only do it by shouting," Victor said. "It's the Latino in him."

"No, it's the father in me," Mimo said. Fortunately they both had lowered their voices. He turned to me. "My brilliant son is going to waste his life as a poet."

"Pablo Neruda's father probably said something similar to him," I said. "Maybe Federico García Lorca's father too. And look how much poorer the world would be without their voices."

"I'm no Neruda or Lorca," Victor said. "But I have a voice that needs to be heard. Poems sing in my heart about the immigrant experience, about being a Jew whose family has wandered for centuries, from the Egyptian desert to the court of Ferdinand and Isabella, to Cuba, to the United States."

"And you can't be an immigration attorney and write poetry on the side?" Mimo demanded. "What about all the refugees who need a strong advocate?"

Rochester tugged on Mimo's pant leg, and the dog's attention calmed the older man, who reached down to pet him.

"Victor told me he's planning to be a teacher who writes poetry," I said. "I've done a lot of teaching myself, and I can tell you it's a valuable profession. Those refugees? Many of them go to school or college here, and so do their children. Victor can have a strong impact on the way they see the world and their success in it."

I looked at him. "The best teachers I know have a way with words that draws in their students. It sounds like you have that. And it's also important to be represented in the classroom, as a man, a Jew, and a person of Latin heritage. Students need to see teachers who are like them."

Rochester sat on his haunches, following the conversation, as I turned back to Mimo. "Teaching is an honorable profession. Think of Rabbi Akiba, Rashi, Maimonides. They led our people in their lifetimes and their words still carry meaning for us. Do you remember the story of the man who asked Rabbi Hillel to state the meaning of Judaism while standing on one foot?"

He glared at me for a moment, but then he lifted his right foot in the air. "Love thy neighbor as thyself," he said.

Rochester woofed in appreciation, which made all three of us laugh and further calmed the tension between father and son.

"Exactly," I said, as he put his foot back down. I turned to Victor. "And why do we remember that story?"

"Because he created a visual image to go with his message," Victor said.

"Just as a poet does! Now please, both of you, can you put aside your arguments and enjoy this family time together? Your sister is here, your cousins, your nieces and nephews."

Mimo opened his arms and Victor stepped into his embrace. "*Te amo, papi,*" Victor said. "I want to make you proud of me."

Rochester circled around them, barking happily and wagging his big plume of a tail.

Mimo stepped back, and put his hands around Victor's face, then kissed his left cheek, and then his right one. "I am always proud of you, *mi hijo.*"

Rochester and I left them and walked back to Lili. "You are a magician," she said. "I'm sure that Mimo and Victor were going to say something neither of them would take back. And look at them now."

Mimo had his arm around Victor's shoulder as they talked to another cousin.

I shrugged. "I understand both their positions. My parents wanted me to be a lawyer, too. Even after I got my MA in English, they still thought I would go to law school." I realized that my eyes were welling up. "I know my father loved me but I'm not sure he was proud of me."

"Because you went to prison?" Lili asked. "Didn't you explain to him why you did what you did?"

"I did. But then he died before I could start over again."

Rochester nuzzled my pant leg, and I reached down to stroke the soft golden hair on his head. My father had always loved dogs, and I knew he'd have fallen for Rochester if they had ever met.

"I'm sure your dad would be proud of what you've accomplished." Lili took my hand and squeezed.

"He'd certainly be proud I was smart enough to marry you," I said.

Food of the Dogs

Rochester barked again in approval as Lili and I kissed, then tried to burrow his way between our legs to be a part of the celebration.

There was a lot of hugging and kissing and many tears shed as Lili's family began to depart. An awful lot of Spanish I didn't understand completely, but I got the drift. They were loving and expressive. I promised myself I'd be more like them in the future.

Most of the guests had left Friar Lake by the time the sun went down, but Rick, Tamsen and Justin hung around to help us clean up. Well, Rick and Tamsen helped, while Justin snoozed on a chair, his dress shirt open at the collar and his tie hanging askew. Rochester slept on the ground next to him, his body curled around the chair legs. Without Justin's own dog, Rascal, there, Rochester had become the ten-year-old's protector

Friar Lake was lovely in the evening gloom. Lights shone from the stained-glass windows of the church and sent colored patterns on the wood dance floor. The DJ and his rig were gone, as well as the caterer and all her equipment.

An owl hooted in the trees, and the moon cast interesting shadows on the lawns. Tamsen collected leftover floral centerpieces and Rick and I folded the chairs and stacked them to make it easier for the company to pick up the next morning. "Try to avoid Brattleboro when you get to Vermont," Rick said. "Try and stay out of hospitals. I read an article this week in a cop journal about a whole department of nurses in a hospital there that were suspended after a bunch of unexplained deaths in the hospital there." He smiled. "Wouldn't want you getting caught up in any investigation when I'm not there to keep an eye on you."

"Fortunately we're going north," I said. "That's where the leaves are supposed to be at their best. I guarantee you I am not going to roam around a hospital in Brattleboro while I'm on my honeymoon."

He laughed. "Famous last words."

Chapter 2
Husband and Wife

By the time we packed everything up, roused Justin and we all drove down the hill from Friar Lake, I was exhausted, and Lili was too. She slumped against the back of the seat with her eyes closed, and even Rochester snoozed in the back.

I took the dog for a quick walk when we got home, and then we collapsed in bed. We were asleep by ten, so that we could get up and out of the house early the next morning.

Because her previous career as a world-class photojournalist involved getting last-minute assignments, Lili was a champ at packing, and the day before the wedding she'd laid out all our clothes on the desk in the office. Even Rochester's food, his bowls, and his traveling water dish were ready to toss into the car.

All we had to do was gather our toiletries and snacks, and we were on our way. Rochester seemed to know this was more than an ordinary trip, and he sat alert on the back seat, his nose making damp prints on the window as he stared out.

I-95 north was so familiar I hardly needed to pay attention. And then the New York State Thruway from the New Jersey border north was flat and dull. The trees had only begun to change color and I was bored of driving, and still coming down from the high of the day before.

"Whose idea was it to drive six hours the day after our wedding?" I asked Lili.

"I think we both thought we could click our heels and say, 'There's no place like Vermont in the fall,' and we'd be there."

Rochester stirred from his place on the back seat and poked his long golden snout between us. "Even the dog is tired of riding in the car, which is saying something," I said.

"Well, at least we're getting off this boring highway," Lili said, peering forward. "According to the directions on my phone we take the next exit to route 149 for route 4."

"Will we be in Vermont then?"

Lili shook her head. "Not for a while yet. New York is a big state."

"How long have we been driving?"

She hit a couple of buttons on her phone. "Four hours."

"Seems like a lifetime," I said.

"And imagine, we have a lifetime ahead of us as husband and wife," Lili said. "And we'll be in Centerbury in another two hours."

"There's that," I said.

We had chosen to honeymoon in Vermont for a number of reasons. First was the opportunity for Lili to photograph the fall foliage. She was looking forward to the interplay of light and colors to take some great pictures. Then she'd contacted a former professor of hers at NYU who was retired and teaching a single course at Centerbury College in the middle of the state.

Professor Eva Alvarez had invited Lili to give a guest lecture to her class on the ethics of photojournalism, a favorite topic of hers. Once we'd settled on Centerbury, I realized that the college had its own conference center up on a mountain, and I'd wangled myself an invitation to visit and share expertise.

I loaded up my Kindle, planning to tackle my mountainous pile of to-be-read books while Lili was off taking pictures. I also scouted out a couple of local hikes Rochester and I could take.

Though Lili had moved in with me two years before the wedding, we were accustomed to leading separate lives during the day and connecting at night, and we thought that was a good plan for the honeymoon.

The landscape improved once we got off the highway. We drove along winding country roads lined with majestic oaks and maples, creating a natural canopy overhead. The trees around us were starting to change colors—hints of red, gold, and orange blending with the lingering greenery. Sunlight filtered through the leaves, casting dappled shadows on the ground.

"This is more like it," Lili said. "It's beautiful. I keep wanting to ask you to pull over so I can take some pictures, but I know there will be so many opportunities."

"There's a scenic overlook ahead," I said. "Why don't we stop there and stretch our legs. I'm sure Rochester can find something to pee on while you take some photos."

I pulled off a few hundred feet later. My forty-year-old legs creaked as I left my enforced sitting posture, but the vista rewarded us. The overlook revealed sweeping views of valleys and mountains covered in colorful foliage against the clear blue sky.

Farms dotted the landscape, their rustic barns and houses providing a country look. Simple wooden fences adorned with seasonal decorations added to the charm. The air carried the scent of fallen leaves, giving a distinct autumn feel.

Rochester was delighted by all the new and different smells, though he was frustrated that I kept him on a leash, limiting his range. A large SUV pulled in beside us and a family spilled out, reminding me of clowns in a circus car. Two parents and four kids, the youngest girl in footed pajamas decorated with Disney princesses.

She had apparently been crying in the car, and her siblings were fed up with her. The older girl and two boys wandered off to look at the view while she stood by the open door of the SUV, sobbing and rubbing her eyes.

Rochester immediately tugged me toward her. The little girl put her arm around his neck and buried her face in his fur. Her parents stood by their SUV, deep in conversation.

"What's the matter, sweetheart?" Lili said, as she knelt beside the girl.

"She left her favorite stuffed dragon at home," the mother said, looking over at us. "She's mad that we won't go back and get it."

The girl looked up at her mother, then at Lili. She spotted the camera around Lili's neck and reached out to touch it. "Will you take my picture?" she asked.

"I'd be happy to," Lili said as she stood up. She began unscrewing a lens on her digital camera.

The girl's mother said, "Come here, sweetheart. Let me comb your hair and wipe your face."

While the mother ministered to the little girl, Lili screwed on a different lens and looked through the viewfinder. Behind them, Rochester walked over to the SUV and began sniffing through the open door.

"Rochester, leave it alone," I called.

"One of the kids probably dropped a snack back there," the father said.

The big golden buried his snout under the front seat, and when he backed out, he had a green-and-purple stuffed dragon in his mouth.

"My dragon!" the little girl said as Rochester brought the toy to her. Decades of breeding to retrieve game had made his jaws gentle.

She burst into a smile as she took the dragon from Rochester, and Lili snapped a series of pictures.

"Say thank you to the nice doggie," the mother said.

She wrapped her arms around his neck and kissed him. "Rochester is good at finding lost things," I said to the mom.

Lili got the dad's email address and promised to forward him the pictures. Then I tugged Rochester to the car and rewarded him with a peanut butter cookie.

We got back on the road, passing farm stands that offered freshly picked apples and homemade goodies. Finally we approached Centerbury, a college town set among the mountains, with steep streets lined with New England style homes.

"This is lovely," Lili said. She looked over at me. "Worth the drive?"

I smiled back at her. "Worth every minute spent with you."

I couldn't help making the comparison with my first wife, Mary. We couldn't have spent so much time in the car without getting into an argument over my driving or something someone had said to her. She said she was allergic to dogs, though I never saw evidence of that, so it goes without saying Rochester wouldn't have been in the picture.

Mary wasn't a big fan of rural settings, either. She was a city girl through and through. She had been raised in Philadelphia and came into her own in New York and Los Angeles. Lili, on the other hand, had been around the world and was able to appreciate her surroundings wherever she was.

Centerbury was stunning in its early autumn attire. The trees were decked in shades of yellow, orange, and red, with bits of green still visible. As we drove along the narrow streets in search of our hotel, we spotted college students in logo sweatshirts hurrying along with heavy backpacks, and a few playing Frisbee on a square of green lawn.

The Otter Creek Inn was a large red-brick building that backed onto the creek, which ran through the center of town. The grounds were filled with tall trees that were already in beautiful color. A crescent driveway was lined with potted chrysanthemums in shades of yellow and orange. Many of the first-floor rooms had French doors, and I hoped we'd be in one of those.

It looked like a lovely place to spend a few days, except for the two men arguing beside a fancy Land Rover SUV.

I pulled up a few feet behind them and got out of the car.

Food of the Dogs

"I'm telling you, this is not the time or the place!" the older man said. He was about seventy, with a distinguished mane of white hair, and he wore a camel hair trench coat.

"This is exactly the time and the place!" the younger man said. He was probably in his forties, and his profile, including a Roman nose, matched the older man. His hair was a light blond, almost white. He wore jeans and a down vest.

I reached in the car and clipped Rochester's leash on him, then let him out. Lili got out of the passenger side and stretched as Rochester tugged me over to one of the chrysanthemums to announce there was a new dog in town.

"You'll regret this!" the younger man said. He got into the SUV, turned it on, and crunched gravel as he tore away.

The older man shook his head, then noticed Rochester. "What a beautiful boy!" he said. He evaluated him. "Purebred golden retriever. Five years old?"

"Very good," I said. I stuck out my hand. "I'm Steve, and this is Rochester."

"It's a habit borne of long experience," the man said. "I trained as a veterinarian, and I've seen a lot of goldens in my time."

He leaned down and scratched behind Rochester's ears, and my dog opened his mouth in pleasure.

"You can call me Dr. M," the man said, when he stood up again. "Everyone does."

"Pleased to meet you," I said. I noticed Lili was getting one of the bags out of the car and I realized I needed to help her. "Are you staying here?"

"We are," Dr. M said. "I thought we had the whole hotel."

"We got a last-minute vacancy," I said. "Well, I'd better help with the bags. Nice to meet you."

He started off down the driveway away from the hotel and I helped Lili finish unloading the bags from the car. "I see Rochester didn't take long to make a new friend," she said.

"Nature of the breed."

We walked up to the front door of the hotel, which was surmounted by a triangular pediment common to old New England buildings. The interior was simple but in elegant taste, with a polished hardwood floor and a fire glowing in a fireplace across from us. We could sit on cushioned benches and look out at the burbling creek later if we chose.

The lobby was empty except for a pony-tailed young woman behind the registration desk. "Are you with the Mihaly party?" she said as we approached. "I thought everyone checked in yesterday."

My heart skipped a beat. Had they screwed up and confirmed a room for Lili when they didn't have one to offer?

"We have a reservation," Lili said politely. "I spoke with Ophelia five days ago and she gave me a confirmation number. I have it here on my phone."

"Well, if you spoke to Ophy then you're fine," the girl said. She pulled out an iPad. "Can I have your number?"

Rochester and I walked over to the bay window that looked out at the creek while Lili checked us in. Two young men paddled a canoe past a man and woman standing beside a pine tree. I couldn't hear what they were saying, but from their body language it looked like they were arguing, too. The woman, who was dressed head-to-toe in black, held a tiny white Bichon in her arms. The man was somewhat younger, with blonde hair like hers but much longer, flowing around his shoulders.

"I have our key," Lili said, as she came over to me. "Our room is right down the hall, and it has French doors so we can duck out easily with Rochester."

I nodded toward the two people. The woman was pointing her finger at the man and appeared to be shouting. "I hope we didn't land in the middle of someone's family feud," I said.

"We are our own family," Lili said. "We don't have to bother with anyone else's."

Chapter 3
Before Your Time

We dumped our bags in the room and headed out to get coffee and a mid-afternoon snack, with Rochester on his leash. From our hilltop perspective, we saw the classic white-steepled church in the town square. It looked like the subject of a charming postcard, with large maple trees framing it on all sides and leaves just starting to turn bright red. In the other direction was a cluster of stone buildings and open lawns.

"Can we head in that direction, toward the college?" Lili asked as we walked. "I'd like to get a sense of where the classroom buildings are before my talk."

"Sure. From the directions I followed to get here, I saw that the street at the bottom of the hill is Main, and that runs right into the campus."

Rochester was eager to sniff each new scent, stopping every few feet to nose out information and leave his pee-mail for other dogs. We didn't mind the slow pace, though, because it gave us the opportunity to take in our surroundings.

"It's nice to get away from our own campus for a while," Lili said. "This is so much more charming than Leighville. It makes the whole area around our campus look almost industrial."

"Well, Leighville started as a factory town," I said. "The college was a relatively late addition, even though it's been around since the early 1900s. Centerbury looks like it grew up more organically around the farms in the area and then the college, and then the tourist trade."

I waved my hand. "There was more wealth here, too. You can tell from the building materials. Here the houses and stores are built from brick and gray stone blocks while back home so many of the building are made of concrete block."

"Not to mention all the historical markers," she said. "So many of these buildings have been around since the Colonial era. And I love all the multi-paned windows and painted shutters. They remind me a bit of that iconic photo of San Francisco, all the gingerbread and the different colors."

We looked at shop displays of college-logo clothes, cell phones, and medical equipment as we strolled. Rochester was happy to sniff his way along the hilly streets. Occasionally I tied his leash to a post so Lili and I could enter one of the charming shops, and I bought him a stuffed otter to play with when we got back to the inn.

We were stopped by a dark-haired, dark-eyed beauty in her early thirties, in a sweatshirt that read "Kiss Me, I'm Greek."

"Hi, I'm Sue, and I run Olives and Feta, a delicious Greek restaurant here in Centerbury," she said, as she handed Lili a flyer. Rochester didn't like something about her, probably the light aroma of something she'd been cooking. His nose was so much more sensitive than mine and sometimes even the faintest scent of something turned him off. He stayed behind me as we looked over the paper.

The top of the page was a photo of a mouthwatering platter of the Greek appetizers called mezes, including olives, blocks of feta, and stuffed grape leaves. Beneath it the text read, "Bring this flyer for a complimentary appetizer with your meal."

"Thank you," Lili said. "We might stop by. Can we bring the dog?"

Food of the Dogs

"He looks sweet and well-behaved," Sue said. "Of course." Then she spotted another couple and moved on.

A few feet later, we stopped at a bookstore with several racks of books out on the pavement. Lili and I stopped to browse there, and Rochester was happy to lie down while we looked. I picked up an older large-format paperback called "What to Feed Your Dog."

I flipped through it. The first section was about puppyhood, the second about the dog's nutritional needs, organized by age and size. "Puppies do best with a balanced diet of nutrients, protein, carbohydrates, and fat," I read. "However, dogs vary in size more than people and need 'size-specific' diets. Great Dane pups grow much faster than Chihuahuas, so they should eat different foods."

That was interesting, and I flipped through to the section about adult dogs, to see if there were any ideas about what I should be feeding Rochester. I was giving him chow recommended by our veterinarian, Dr. Horz, and while I trusted her I was open to new ideas.

I got sidetracked by a diagram of a dog's digestive tract and was reading closely when Lili joined me. "If you like that so much then buy it," she said. "I want to get that coffee. And I could do with some sugar."

I kissed her. "There's the sugar," I said, and she laughed.

I walked inside and handed the twenty-something clerk the book. His name tag read Ethan, and he looked like the kind of guy who came to school at Centerbury and never left. Leighville was full of Eastern grads and Eastern dropouts who fell in love with the area and stayed.

"Five dollars," he said. He looked behind me at Rochester, waiting with Lili. "Beautiful dog you have."

"Thank you. He's a sweetheart."

"You're visiting?"

I nodded, as I handed him a bill. "Leaf-peeping for a week."

"If you're still here on Friday you'll have to bring your dog to the opening of the new dog park," he said. "That is, if the town lets it open."

"There's a problem?"

He sighed. "There's always a problem in small towns," he said. "Rich guy who used to live here came back to see a property he still owned, which was run into the ground by the last owners. He had the building razed and decided to donate the land to the town."

"That's nice."

"Yeah, but some of the neighbors don't want a dog park there. Barking, people not picking up their dogs' poop, that kind of complaint. And the rich guy trampled over their feelings and people say he paid someone off. Personally, I think it'll be great. I've got a basset hound and I'm looking forward to taking her there."

"I'm not sure we'll be in town, but if we are, I'll stop by with Rochester."

Ethan looked at me. "After the character in *Jane Eyre*?"

"Got it in one. Most people think of the city, or Jack Benny's sidekick."

"Don't know who Jack Benny is. One of those late-night talk show hosts?"

"Before your time." I picked up the bag with the book in it. "Have a good day."

I walked out to Lili. "I feel old." I told her about the clerk who didn't know who Jack Benny was.

"You're not old, you have a specialized frame of reference." She linked her arm in mine and we kept walking. I did have a special set of skills—with Rochester's help, I'd helped Rick solve a series of crimes in Stewart's Crossing. I had the computer knowledge to dig deep into the dark web for information and motivation, and my dog's big nose and curious mind had led to the discovery of many clues.

But we were on vacation, and I wasn't going to go looking for another crime to solve.

Chapter 4
Ophelia Recommends

We stopped at a café with outdoor tables and ordered big steaming mugs of café mocha along with a couple of croissants. From the bakery case I picked out a biscuit for Rochester in the shape of a bone, decorated with pink dots.

Though the air was chilly, the late-afternoon sun warmed us as much as the coffee. We sat there watching the traffic, drinking our coffee and eating our croissants as Rochester wolfed his biscuit down. The air was filled with the smell of pumpkin and apple pies, and the buildings around us had a charming look. All around us were pretty New England homes, white clapboards with wooden shutters and slanted roofs. A pair of tween girls raced past us, one on a bike with pink tassels and the other on a foot-propelled scooter.

It was a perfect, sunny yet brisk autumn day, though I knew there would be a long, punishing Vermont winter ahead. By then, though, we'd be back in Stewart's Crossing, where it did get cold, but snowed infrequently.

We finished our croissants and made our way back to the inn, noting a number of restaurants that looked good. "Feel like moussaka for dinner?" Lili asked. "We have that coupon."

"It's all Greek to me."

She groaned. "We can ask the people at the inn for advice."

"That teenager at reception? She looks like she lives on pizza and diet Coke."

"I meant the owners," Lili said. "That woman I made the reservation with, Ophelia? She said she could help with any information we need."

As we approached the inn, a car with Wisconsin plates zoomed past us and turned sharply into the parking space beside my SUV. An older man and woman got out, the driver barely avoiding slamming his door into my car. They stalked inside, neither of them speaking.

They had already gone to their room by the time we entered the quiet lobby. A slim woman sat by the fire, with a fluffy Bichon on her lap. I recognized her as one of the two I'd seen arguing outside earlier.

As soon as he saw Rochester, the Bichon jumped up and started a high-pitched rapid bark. The woman put her hand on his back.

"Ming Chow, be nice." She called "Sorry," in our direction, then stood up with the dog in her arms and walked toward the hallway that led to the rooms.

The teenager who'd checked us in was gone, replaced by a cheerful plump woman in a low-necked blouse that revealed a sprawling tattoo. "Are you Ophelia?" Lili asked.

"I am. You must be Mr. and Mrs. Levitan."

"I'm Lili and this is Steve. Do you have any recommendations for dinner?"

"Normally we serve in our dining room, but because of the big party we have we're doing custom menus for them," she said. "Mountain House does great steaks. If you like Italian, I can recommend L'Osteria down the street or Olives and Feta for Greek. You can take your dog there."

"We got a flyer for that Greek place this afternoon from a woman named Sue," I said. "While we were out walking."

"Sue Flocky and her husband Aristotle opened Olives and Feta a year ago. If you like Greek food, they're the best. They're struggling to build a business." She sighed. "Tyson and I know what they're going through. Business in Centerbury is seasonal, though at least we have several seasons. Some of them are tied to the college—move in, graduation, and so on. And we get hikers in the summer and skiers in the winter, though not as much as some places."

"What's the big party you have?" I asked. "Family reunion? We just got married and we had one of those. Though a lot more people than you can accommodate here."

"I come from a big family," Lili said.

"It's a mixed group," Ophelia said. "Family-owned business, so most of the people are related, though there are a few employees as well. Doctor M's Fine Dog Food."

"That's the company? I met Dr. M when we came in."

"He's a sweetheart. He raised his family here in Centerbury and coming back is a reunion for him and his son Alistair and his children as well as a board meeting for his company. He was in the hospital recently, too, so he's celebrating getting better."

She leaned on the counter. "It's a bit of a strain on us, though, having such a big group. They all want to eat at the same time, they're all out of their rooms in meetings at the same time. That kind of thing. But we're managing. At least I got them to agree to a custom dinner menu with two choices, rather than having to manage cooking the whole menu at once."

"You're the chef?" Lili asked.

"Chief cook and bottle washer. My husband Tyson keeps the property going, supervises the maids and he keeps the grounds up." She smiled. "This has been our dream. We met in Brooklyn and one of the things that made us fall in love was that we both wanted to have a country inn."

"That's lovely," Lili said. "You chose a beautiful property."

"It wasn't anything like it is now when we bought it. It was a rundown old coaching inn from the 1800s and it needed a complete overhaul. We sunk way too much money into fixing it up and we're struggling to keep our head above water." She smiled. "But you know how it is with dreams. You have to work to make them come true."

I took Lili's hand. "It was a lot of work to plan our wedding, and we're still together, so I know what you mean."

She shook her head. "I was only going to walk away from you twice during that planning."

I opened my mouth in mock horror. "Only twice? I was ready to quit at least three times."

She knocked me on the shoulder with her fist. "My husband, the comedian," she said. Then she stopped. "Oh, wow. That's the first time I've used that phrase in a long time."

"I'm husband number three," I said to Ophelia. "She's wife number two."

"Tyson and I are each other's first," Ophelia said. "I hope we can keep it that way."

"How long have you been open?" Lili asked.

"This is our third year. We were lucky to book such a big party this week—the peak date for leaf-peeping is still about ten days away. But Dr. M's party pushes us into profitability for the first time since we opened. We might be able to start taking salaries soon."

"You don't pay yourselves?" I asked.

Ophelia shook her head. "Fortunately Tyson has a small inheritance from his grandmother that helps us keep our heads above water. We pay our staff first, then our bills. Insurance keeps going up, and so do taxes. But this is a dream for both of us so we're willing to sacrifice while we're young."

"The hotel is lovely," Lili said. "You must be doing something right."

"I hope so," Ophelia said, and then the phone rang and she had to answer it.

We both agreed with her, then went back to our room to relax and unpack. Rochester snoozed on the carpet, lying on his side with his legs splayed out, as if he'd picked the spot in the room where he could cause the most trouble as we walked around him.

We decided on L'Osteria. Rochester was tired from the long trip and I knew he'd snooze contentedly in the room while we were out.

I sprawled on the bed for a while, looking through the book I'd bought. "Look at this picture on the back," I said, holding the book up to her. "Doesn't this look like the old guy I was talking to earlier?"

"I didn't see him."

"He said his name was Dr. M, and that's the name of the company that reserved the rooms. This author's last name is Mihaly."

"Then it might be him."

"Cool. Maybe I can have him autograph the book. And see what advice he has for feeding Rochester."

At that moment, the dog looked up from the floor. "You said the F word," Lili said. "Time for you to put out his food, and for us to get dinner."

I poured kibble into a bowl and laid a bowl of water beside it. Rochester looked at it from his position, did a trial sniff, then went back to sleep.

"So much for that." We grabbed our coats and I turned to the dog. "Try not to destroy anything while we're gone."

Chapter 5
Rochester and Jane

The temperature had dropped while we were inside, and we hurried down the hill to L'Osteria. I worried it would be a generic Italian restaurant specializing in pizza and calzones, but I was pleasantly surprised to see not only Italian standards but the chef's interpretation of less familiar dishes.

Our waitress, a petite brunette named Winnie, welcomed us, and recommended the bruschetta as an appetizer. "Chef's version is more like a flatbread, with sundried tomatoes and olives."

"Sounds great."

"Our house white wine is a pinot grigio from Alto Adige. Would you like to try it?"

"We'll take two glasses," Lili said.

When Winnie came back with the wine, we ordered the fried calamari as an appetizer. I chose the tortellini in a rich chicken broth flavored with saffron, while Lili ordered chicken piccata with capers and artichoke hearts.

Since the restaurant wasn't busy, Winnie seemed willing to linger, and I asked her, "Have you lived in Centerbury long?"

"My whole life," she said. "It's a nice town but things move slowly. Most exciting thing to happen here of late has been a dog park."

"Plenty of excitement for the dog owners, I imagine."

"Oh sure. We were all surprised when old Doc Mihaly decided to come back to town and reclaim his old vet clinic."

Lili's ears perked up at the town gossip. "Why were people surprised?"

Winnie leaned in, excited to dish. "Doc sold the clinic years ago to his assistant, but held onto the property. Then there was some bad business that turned people against dogs being there. Rumor was the land was cursed."

I shared a puzzled glance with Lili. "Cursed land? What happened exactly?"

"It's pretty sad," Winnie said. "The assistant who bought from Doc Mihaly ended up euthanizing himself there after some dogs died under his care."

We digested this news as Winnie went to put in our dinner order. "That's a very odd way to say things, isn't it?" Lili asked.

"It is. I don't believe in curses," I said. "But I am curious about the veterinary practice. I can see why people in a small town would shy away from a vet who made errors that resulted in the loss of someone's dog."

The revelations about the land cast a somber mood in the air, despite the aromatic Italian food. "You'd more than shy away," Lili said. "You'd sue. You'd stand outside with a protest sign if anything happened to Rochester."

"*Chas v'shalom*," I said. "At least that's what mother used to say in Yiddish, in place of God forbid. Or in our case, dog forbid."

"My mother would say *Dios no lo quiera*," Lili said. "Something like God doesn't want that."

"I was surprised at how much I understood your relatives, even when they were speaking Spanish," I said. "The cultural connection was so strong. The Judaism overwhelmed the language differences."

"I've always walked between those worlds," Lili said. "The Spanish and the Jewish. How my father thought his family was discriminated against in Cuba because they weren't Sephardic. He never felt comfortable being Ashkenazi there. I think he was grateful that Castro's regime gave him an excuse to leave."

We left the restaurant feeling full in stomach yet mystified about the town's undercurrents surrounding dogs, land deals, and the Mihaly family. When we returned to the inn, I took Rochester out for his after-dinner walk and we ran into the man in the camel hair trenchcoat, Dr. M. He was walking an elderly female golden with a shaggy coat that glowed amber in the streetlight.

She immediately lay down on the pavement and rolled onto her back. "Rochester, be nice," I said.

Dr. M looked at me. "Your dog's name is Rochester?"

"Indeed. He was a rescue, and he came with that name."

"Well, it's just perfect, because my girl's name is Janie," he said. "And in the book, they end up together."

"Well, yes, but Rochester has to be blinded and disfigured first," I said. "I'd rather keep him whole and tied to me. And besides, he was neutered, so nothing can come of a relationship."

"Yes, Janie was neutered too," he said, as Rochester sniffed her and she batted at his nose with her paw. Then she jumped up and they played for a minute.

She got tired quickly, though, and she sat on her hind legs next to the doctor. "How old is Janie?" I asked.

"She's twelve. She has some arthritis in her legs, and I'm watching her kidney functions, but otherwise she's a sweet, healthy girl."

"Rochester is only five, and we've had an easy time with him," I said. "He's very loving and curious." I didn't need to mention that his curiosity extended to helping me and my police detective friend Rick solve crimes. That was between the three of us—well, four, if you included Lili.

"It must be nice to get all of your family together," I said, as Dr. M and Janie walked back to the inn with us. It had gotten even chillier as night fell, and I picked up the collar of my coat to shield my throat.

"I've got a bit of a heart condition, and I ended up in the hospital a few weeks ago in Brattleboro. I was doing a promotional tour for the company, showing the products off to veterinarians, and I overdid things a bit."

He smiled, but the edges of his mouth didn't turn up as we turned a corner and began the climb to the inn. "That encouraged me to bring everyone here to Centerbury for our corporate meeting. It would be better if we all got along," he said. "It's my fault, really. I started my business a few years ago and it has been very successful, and I brought both my children in to help. So on top of our general family drama, we have business problems to confront, and right now my son and I are at loggerheads."

In the distance, a car passed, the air filling with the loud bass line of electronic dance music, the kind kids played out of dorm room windows at Eastern.

"What kind of business?" I asked, when the music passed. "Writing? Earlier today I was at the bookstore in town and I bought a book I think you wrote."

"I did indeed write that. I've been a veterinarian for most of my career," he said. "About ten years ago I started noticing differences in Janie's behavior based on the food I was feeding her. I did some research and created my own formula. It had a dramatic effect on her health, so I wrote the book. Based on the success of that, I raised some capital and started a business."

I nodded. "I've seen your brand of food at the vet's office, but I haven't tried it."

He had to stop for a moment to catch his breath. The steep climb was getting to me, too, though I was at least twenty-five years younger.

"Our distribution has been focused on veterinary offices," he said. "I go to conventions and write articles for magazines, and that convinces vets to give the food a try. As soon as they see the effect on their patients, they're sold and become distributors."

"Sounds like a good operation."

We started to climb again. "My son wants to expand to retail stores as well as build an online store to sell direct to customers." Maybe the catch in his breath was due to the climb, or his disagreement with his son, but there was some tension there.

"I'm no businessman, but that sounds like a good idea. I'm always looking for people I can trust to help me take better care of Rochester."

We reached the front door of the inn, and I was grateful to get inside out of the cold. "In principle it's a great idea," Dr. M continued. "But I'm worried that if we grow too quickly our supply chain won't be able to keep up. And in addition to the canine vitamins we add, we use real, human-quality ingredients like chicken, beef, and salmon. The more we need, the higher the price we'll have to pay."

I nodded. "And that pushes up your retail price."

We both opened our coats against the warmth of the lobby. "Indeed. Alistair has suggested that we outsource production to a foreign country where the costs are lower, but I'm worried that the quality will suffer." He shook his head. "It's an intractable problem made worse because of the father-son dynamic."

We bid our goodnights and as Rochester and I went back to our room, I thought about my relationship with my father. He was an engineer, and he approached every problem logically. He didn't believe in making decisions based on emotion.

That was tough for me as a teenager, when I was filled with confusion, hormones, and indecision. I was too worried about what a girl said to me, or an upcoming test, to stack the dishes the way he preferred in the dishwasher. He was obsessed with opening boxes correctly, and if I ripped open the ice cream carton to get to my peppermint stick quickly, he had a fit.

At one point in my teens I was obsessed with architecture, and I dragged my parents from New Castle, Delaware to Tarrytown, New York, to see historic homes and modern ones, buildings I read about in magazines and whole towns that had retained their 18th century flavor. When I was bored in high school classes, I sketched house designs and I was sure I wanted to be an architect.

My father worked hard to disabuse me of that idea. "You don't have the discipline for architecture," he said. "It's a lot of math and engineering. And you can barely draw a straight line."

I protested that I could use a ruler, but my lack of talent for high school algebra and geometry eventually doomed me, even though I joined the Mathletes and struggled through competition problems.

He was probably relieved when I majored in English at Eastern, because he and my mother had determined that I ought to go to law school. Then my mother went to work as a secretary at a law firm, and got me a summer job proofreading there. Seeing how local attorneys worked turned me off on that career, but I didn't tell my parents.

Most of my fellow English majors at Eastern College were heading to law school or graduate school, or taking time off to "clear their heads." My head was clear enough, and I wanted to live in the big city, so when I was accepted at Columbia University for the MA in English, I signed right up. My parents realigned their ideas to think of me as a tenured professor with a PhD in some obscure area of literature. Then once again I probably disappointed them by taking a series of jobs as a technical writer.

Seeing Lili waiting for me in our hotel room banished all thoughts of my past. As Rochester often reminded me, I needed to live in the moment. And I was a man on his honeymoon with the woman he loved.

"I wish we could stay like this forever," Lili said, propping herself up on one elbow to watch me as I unwound my scarf, stuffed my gloves in my pocket, and took off my parka.

"No, you don't," I said. "You're a type A personality. You need to take pictures, teach, and run the Fine Arts department. And occasionally take a nice vacation."

"I suppose. You'd get bored, too, after a few days, without something to snoop into."

I joined her on the bed, and took her hand, running my thumb over her new wedding band. "I promise to be the husband you deserve, Lili. I've learned from my past mistakes. You and me, we're a team now."

Rochester jumped on the bed and walked between us, not caring who he stepped on. Lili smiled. "A team with a very bossy mascot. Fortunately I love Rochester, so I don't mind sharing you with him."

He snuggled down between us, and I read on my Kindle, one hand on the dog and the other to turn the pages. It was very sweet, the three of us together, not distracted by any college drama or case for Rochester and me to investigate.

Rochester eventually snoozed, his chest rising and falling with light snores. Then, like clockwork, he sprung up at ten o'clock, ready for his last walk before bedtime.

I wanted to lie in bed with Lili, letting my body rebuild the store of dopamine it had just depleted, but Rochester wanted his bedtime walk. Grudgingly, I put my clothes back on, layering a sweater under my parka for extra warmth.

As we walked out into the hotel lobby, my heart felt full. Lili understood me in a way no one else ever had. She saw past my flaws and failings to the man I wanted to be. With her by my side, I knew we could weather any storm - solving murders or building a life together.

Then my adrenaline spiked because Ming Chow's mom was screaming at Ophelia at the front desk. "My dog is missing!" she said. "You have to help me find her! Send out the maids and the bellmen and whoever you have."

Chapter 6
Disagreeable

"It's late, Miss Mihaly," Ophelia said politely. "Our staff have already gone home. It's just me and my husband, but we can help you look."

"My golden and I can help," I said. "The white Bichon who was with you earlier?"

She turned to me and nodded. "Ming Chow," she said. "He's my emotional support dog. He almost never leaves me."

"When did you last see him?" I asked. I tried to keep my voice calm, to bring down the woman's anxiety level. Rochester is usually good at calming people, but he stayed behind me, probably frightened by her combination of fear and agitation.

"He was in my room. I went to talk to Beverly, one of my dad's employees, in her room, and I didn't want to take Ming Chow with me because she was very fretful."

"Could Ming Chow still be in your room?"

"I searched everywhere, even in the closet and under the bed." She turned to Ophelia. "You really need to have the maid dust under there."

Rochester lowered his head and emitted a soft growl. He didn't like it when people were rude.

"I'll take care of it tomorrow morning," Ophelia said.

"Could Ming Chow have slipped out somehow?" I asked. "He's a small dog." I had helped Rick with the theft of several dogs of Ming Chow's size back home in Stewart's Crossing. Even if they weren't stolen, they could slip through gates and tiny openings.

"I left the sliding door open just an inch, so he could have fresh air," Zoe said. "Oh, God, what if someone stole him? His parents were both show dogs and I paid thousands of dollars for him."

She looked around the empty hotel lobby. "You don't know what's going on with these meetings my father is forcing us to have. People are getting cutthroat. I wouldn't be surprised if someone stole him just to get back at me. My brother, for one. He knows how much Ming Chow means to me."

"Rochester and I will take a look around the outside of the inn," I said. "He probably sniffed another dog or something interesting. I'll bet he's close by."

Ophelia stepped around from behind the desk. "Come with me. I'll help you look around inside."

Rochester and I walked out the front door, and a strong wind whipped cold air across my face. Normally I'd have hurried Rochester along, especially since Lili was waiting in bed for me. But I couldn't let a dog go missing.

Rochester sniffed at each chrysanthemum and holly bush we passed, his whole snout quivering as he used his whiskers to evaluate the world. I'd learned that dog whiskers were more sensitive than regular hairs, almost like a human's fingertips. They conveyed a lot of information back to his brain.

But Ming Chow wasn't lurking behind the chrysanthemums or under the hedges. "We're looking for that little Bichon," I reminded him. "I hope he'll start to bark again as soon as he figures out you're around."

Instead of heading down the sidewalk as we usually would, I let Rochester take the lead, and we traipsed across the dry grass, past the line of rooms that faced the street. Ours was on the other side of the building, but many of these rooms had French doors like ours did.

"I should have asked which way her room faced," I said, as Rochester kept his nose to the ground.

Though Rochester stopped to pee occasionally, he didn't signal anything unusual. I suppressed a laugh as I envisioned him returning to the lobby with Ming Chow in his jaws, the way he'd delivered the stuffed dragon to the little girl.

We came to the end of the building and turned the corner. Through the glass exit door I saw Ophelia and Zoe in the hallway. The dog's mother appeared to be losing it, alternately yelling and crying. No wonder she needed an emotional support dog.

I saw a burly guy in jeans and a plaid shirt shining a flashlight under the bushes that ran between the inn and the row of houses that sprawled down the hill. "Looking for Ming Chow?" I asked.

He looked up at me. "Yup. You, too?"

I nodded. "I'm Steve, and this is Rochester."

He stuck out a hand to me. "I'm Tyson. Ophelia and I own the inn. This isn't the way we usually hope to welcome guests."

"It's no problem. Rochester loves to find things. Unfortunately, we're not having much luck."

"I'm going to head toward the creek," Tyson said. "Maybe the little dog wanted a drink. I just hope he didn't fall in. There's a current that heads down toward the falls on the other side of town. That would be a pretty rough ride for a little guy, especially with that big tumble."

Tyson went down the hill, and Rochester and I continued a circuit around the Inn, sticking close to the building. We stayed out there for another half hour, and then it started to rain. "I don't think we're going to have much success in this weather, puppy," I said. I tugged on his leash. "Let's get inside."

While I felt bad about the missing dog, I was sure that he would show up on his own, and Lili, Rochester and I went to sleep.

Chapter 7
On the Hunt

Tuesday morning I took Rochester out for a quick walk in the crisp sunshine. When we returned to the hotel I spotted a display of muffins, croissants, and Danish pastries. Ophelia was setting up canisters of regular and decaf coffee and a tray of croissants and baby Danish. Her hair was pulled back into a loose ponytail and she looked tired.

"Sorry I'm running a little late this morning, didn't get much sleep last night," she said. "Tyson and I were up for hours looking for the lost dog."

"He still didn't show up?" I asked. "Rochester and I can help again today if you'd like."

"That would be great. Once the Mihaly group is in the conference room, we need to do a full sweep of the interior of the inn. And if he's not here, we'll have to start another search outside, too."

I looked out the window to the creek. "At least it's a nice day," I said. "I hope the poor puppy got some shelter from the rain last night."

"I hope so, too. Tyson and I both got soaked through while we were looking."

I hurried back to the room. "Breakfast in the lobby," I told Lili.

"Are you sure it's for us?" Lili asked. "It could be for the people who rented out the hotel, that doctor and his family."

"The Inn's website read bed and breakfast," I said. "And we're registered guests."

Rochester accompanied us back to the lobby, and I grabbed a croissant from the display and gave it to him to keep him occupied. Lili and I loaded paper plates with pastries and then we sat at one end of the single long table, Rochester on the floor beside us.

A number of other guests sat at the other end of the table, talking together. I recognized Alistair Mihaly and a woman I assumed was his wife. They had their heads together, talking quietly.

I didn't see Zoe Mihaly and wondered if she was already up and out looking for Ming Chow. Or maybe she was so stressed out that she was sleeping in. I knew that if Rochester was missing I wouldn't be able to sleep.

A statuesque Black woman sat down beside Lili. She was in late middle-age, in a trim business suit that contrasted with Lili's and my LL Bean vacation outfits. "You must be the replacements for Frank and Joan," she said, in a gentle Caribbean accent. "I'm Beverly."

We introduced ourselves. "Who are Frank and Joan?" I asked.

"Frank is one of our board members," Beverly said. "Sorry, I should have started with an introduction. We're all affiliated with Dr. M's Healthy Dog Foods. I'm the corporate secretary. Everyone here is either a family member or an employee or both. We had reserved the whole inn, but Frank came down with a respiratory illness the other day and we canceled their room."

"Our good luck," Lili said. "We were so caught up with wedding plans that we didn't make any honeymoon reservations. We were able to take over that last room."

"Well, I hope we won't interfere with your visit," Beverly said. "Things tend to get contentious when we all get together. But we'll try to keep that within the meeting room."

"I talked to Dr. M last night as we were walking our dogs," I said.

"He mentioned there was a difference of opinion about how to grow the company."

Beverly nodded. "Dr. M is happy with the way things are. The business income supplements his retirement. But Alistair wants to build his own empire. They're both very strong-willed men, so I have no idea how it will all wash out."

Another woman approached and sat down across from Beverly, and the two of them got into a conversation. Lili and I finished breakfast and went back to our room. "The dog's still missing," I said to Lili as I walked in.

Rochester came up close to me as he smelled the fresh pastry. "I said I'd take the dog and help look, if you don't mind going out driving on your own."

"I figured you'd want to stay here and read," she said. "So I don't mind driving. There's a pretty covered bridge I want to check out. And I found an online source that said the trees in Vergennes are in full color, and I can pass the bridge on the way."

"Sounds like a plan," I said. "I'll let you know if we find the dog, and maybe we can rendezvous later."

She left, and a few minutes later, I walked back to the lobby with Rochester, ready to start searching. Zoe Mihaly was arguing with her father and the man I'd seen her outside with the day before. "You can't just go into that meeting while Ming Chow is missing!" she said. "You have to help look for him."

"The dog will show up, Zoe," the man said.

"You don't know that, Win!" she said. "Someone could have dognapped him. He's a valuable purebred." She put her hands on her hips. "You didn't take him, did you? Just to be mean? Or maybe you've already sold him."

"Children, please," Dr. M said. "Zoe, you know your brother would never take your dog."

"He did when we were kids," she said. "Remember Wheeler?"

"Wheeler was a stuffed dog," Dr. M said. "Not a live one. And he only hid him to make you cry."

"It is exactly the same thing!"

Alistair put his arm around Zoe. "Come on, sis. The innkeepers said they'll keep looking. You come into the meeting with us, and they'll let us know when they find him."

Ophelia was behind the desk, and she called out, "That's true, Miss Mihaly. Tyson and I will find your dog."

Zoe let herself be led through a door at the far end of the lobby. "At least she's not going around with us," she said to me. "Last night she was so anxious I had to spend half my time calming her down."

"What can we do to help?" I asked.

"Tyson and I will check each of the guest rooms," she said. "But if you and Rochester could look through the rest of the property, that would be great. And if he's not inside, we'll make a plan to search outside."

Ophelia's husband came out from the office behind the lobby. "Here's a master key to all the rooms except the guests," he said. He handed it to me, along with a paper sketch of the building. "This will show you where everything is."

"Thanks. We'll do our best."

Rochester and I started in the kitchen. It made sense to me that the little dog might have smelled food and snuck in there, and then gotten stuck behind a piece of equipment. As I expected, the kitchen was cozy and well-organized, with the requisite food-safety posters and a couple of framed needlepoint sayings like "No matter where life takes us, we always return to the kitchen."

I closed the door behind me and let Rochester off his leash to sniff around. "Remember, we're looking for the little Bichon," I said. "Not food."

He opened his mouth with a wide grin and then went nose to the ground. A commercial-grade electric stove with six burners and a large oven sat against one wall. Above it were racks of saucepans, stockpots and other kitchen tools.

I opened the spacious refrigerator and freezer though I certainly didn't hope to find a frozen dog there. All I saw were neatly labeled perishable ingredients and pre-prepared items. Beside the fridge was a long stainless steel prep table, with a large, wall-mounted microwave oven. Two wooden knife blocks rested to one side.

Next to that was a large, deep sink for washing dishes and a separate, smaller sink for handwashing and food preparation. Storage shelves beside that, filled with dry goods, dishes and glassware.

Around the corner was a commercial dishwasher. More tools hung on pegs above it-- spatulas, ladles, whisks. Then another table with a large toaster and an array of boxed coffee and tea products. I figured that the urns which were out in the lobby at the moment belonged there.

Rochester nosed his way along the floor, sniffing beside equipment and trying to get behind it. I listened carefully for any sound of Ming Chow but couldn't hear anything.

We finally gave up, and worked our way through the office, the staff restroom, and the laundry room. I looked in each washer and dryer, and Rochester sniffed everywhere, but we came up empty-handed and empty-pawed.

Things were not looking good for a safe return for the little Bichon. But I refused to give up searching until he was found.

Chapter 8
Slipped Out?

Lili sent me a text with a photo of the covered bridge, and I responded that Rochester and I were still searching. I didn't think the bridge was that attractive, but she had found a unique and flattering angle. That was her talent, harnessing the power of light and shadow, framing her shots in ways that enhanced the way she wanted you to feel.

Rochester and I walked back out to the lobby where we found Zoe Mihaly on her cell phone. She quickly ended the call and turned to me. "Did you find him?"

I shook my head.

"You have to understand why Ming Chow is so important to me. My family was pretty dysfunctional when I was a kid, and I was lucky that my father was a vet," she said. "We always had dogs and cats and rabbits and guinea pigs. Half the time when a pet was abandoned my dad would bring it home, and I'd be the one to take care of it."

She sniffled and wiped her eyes. "My mom was sick a lot and then she died. Alistair is a stuck-up prick and Winston is a loser so laid back I'm surprised his head doesn't hit the floor. It's no wonder I ended up on drugs."

"I'm sorry," I said. "Difficult childhoods are tough to overcome."

She nodded. "I'm much better now that I have Ming Chow. And for the first time I'm working at a job I enjoy, marketing for the company. I set up all my dad's appointments with vets and speaking engagements, and I create and place all the ads in veterinary journals. Alistair wants to change our whole approach and aim for the mass market, and my dad and I are always arguing with him. Ming Chow helps me stay calm."

"We're going to keep looking," I said. "Ophelia and Tyson are going through the guest rooms and Rochester and I have been through all the back of house."

"I'm afraid either Alistair or Win have taken him, to destabilize me and undermine my position about the marketing."

"Does your brother Win also work for the company?"

She shook her head. "He's just waiting for Daddy to keel over so he can inherit and stay a ski bum for the rest of his life. He's only here because he wants Daddy to retire and hand over some part of the company to each of us."

Beverly came to the door of the conference room. "Zoe?" she called. "We're taking a vote and we need you here."

"You go," I said. "We'll keep looking."

She went back into the conference room, and Tyson came out from the hallway that led to the guest rooms. "No luck there," he said. "You find anything?"

I shook my head.

"I'm afraid the dog slipped out through the French doors," he said. "We tell the guests to keep them locked but if the weather is nice sometimes they leave them open a crack for fresh air."

"You don't think someone dognapped Ming Chow?" I asked. "It sounds like Zoe's relationship with her brothers is rocky."

"That's always possible, but I want to do a better search outside now that it's daylight and not raining. Can you help?"

"Absolutely."

He brought out a paper map of Centerbury from behind the

front desk and showed me where the Inn was. He drew a rough circle around the property, and divided it into halves. "I already looked by the creek last night, but because of the rain I might have missed something," he said.

"We'll head down there."

It was midmorning by then. Lili texted that she'd stopped to get a snack in Vergennes, and asked how the hunt was going. She accompanied the message with more photos of trees in vibrant colors and a couple of heart emojis. It made me feel great to know that I was giving her this experience. I hoped we'd be able to share more time together as the week progressed.

Tyson's directions had me start at the side of the inn adjacent to a row of houses with steep, pitched roofs and symmetrical facades, many of them with two multi-pane windows on each side of a doorway with a pediment over it. They were built of horizontal wooden planks that overlap slightly, painted in pale colors with wooden shutters in darker colors.

Rochester sniffed his way down the street, stopping occasionally to anoint a bush or wrought iron fence. I called, "Ming Chow! Here, boy!" several times but got no response. I stopped a couple of people on the street but no one had seen a fluffy white dog.

A bridge crossed the creek at the bottom of the hill, and Rochester and I turned back up along the bank toward the inn. Rochester tugged me down toward the water, which burbled in the sunshine, glinting as the current rushed past. I hoped Ming Chow hadn't fallen in. With his short paws he couldn't be much of a swimmer and he might be swept down toward the rapids and the falls farther downstream.

Then I heard a whimper, and glimpsed white fur in the roots and weeds along the creek bank. As we got closer, I saw that Ming Chow had gotten his pink harness caught in a tree root and he couldn't get away.

He began yipping in terror as Rochester and I approached. "You stay back, puppy," I said to my dog, and I leaned down to free Ming

Chow. The little beast snapped at me and I had to keep my hand away from his sharp teeth as I struggled to disconnect the harness from the tree's grasp.

By the time I freed him he was in a full frenzy. I lifted him by the harness and cradled him in one arm. I used the other hand to grasp Rochester's leash and we hurried back to the inn.

He was wet and dirty, and Zoe Mihaly wasn't going to be happy. I walked over to the door to the conference room, knocked briefly and stuck my head in.

"I found Ming Chow."

Zoe jumped up from her seat and came running. "Oh, my poor baby." She looked at me. "What did you do to him?"

She took the dog from me, getting her white cashmere sweater wet and dirty.

I resented the implication that I was responsible for his sorry state but I kept my temper. "He was caught in some roots by the river," I said. "Lucky Rochester and I found him or he could have gone down over the falls."

"This horrible town," she said. "I hated it when I lived here and I hate having to come back here." She stalked away toward her room without thanking me or Rochester for bringing her baby back to her.

Ophelia came into the lobby then. "Thank you for your help," she said. "I'll bet your boy was the one who found him." She walked behind the registration desk and pulled out a dog biscuit. "I don't know how tasty these are, but Dr. M brought us a whole bag of them."

She handed the biscuit to Rochester, who chewed it briefly and then wolfed it down.

"I guess he likes them," I said.

She gave me a couple, and we headed back to the room. My parka was damp and dirty and I wanted to clean the creek water off. As we did, I wondered how Ming Chow had gotten out of Zoe's room. Had she accidentally left the door open? Or had someone come along from the outside and opened it, hoping to snatch him up?

Chapter 9
A Tourist in Town

I texted Lili that we'd found the dog, and she replied that she was on her way back to Centerbury. Rochester slumped by the bed and I picked up my Kindle to read. Lili found us that way when she returned.

We went out for lunch with Rochester, and found a café not too far from the Inn where we could stop. On the way home, he stopped to sniff a bush, but he was taking an awfully long time. "What's up, boy?" I asked. "We already found Ming Chow."

He looked up at me and then his head went back down, and he grabbed a piece of paper in his jaws. I squatted beside him. "What do you have?" I asked as I scratched under his jaw and his mouth opened. He dropped the crumpled piece of paper and I picked it up. It was on the letterhead of a law firm and read, "Petition to determine incapacity in the matter of Dr. Anthony Mihaly."

I smoothed it out, but the rest of the page had been torn off and that was all I could read. As we walked back, I recalled Dr. M telling me that he'd had heart problems recently and been hospitalized in Brattleboro. Was that what this was about? Perhaps a preventative measure to maintain control of the business if Dr. M had experienced complications in the hospital, or needed extra time to recuperate?

Or was it something more? Alistair and Dr. M had argued the evening before. Was his son trying to tell him he wasn't sharp enough to run the business anymore? Dr. M had complained that Alistair wanted to expand the business, though his father had concerns. Was Alistair trying to get his dad out of the way so he could do what he wanted?

The night before, Lili said I wouldn't be happy on a vacation without something to investigate. Maybe I was just inventing problems, and needed to focus on my honeymoon instead.

"What did you think of Doctor M?" Lili asked as we continued back to the Inn.

"I liked him," I said. "But of course I'm prejudiced toward anyone who likes goldens."

"Have you heard about his food before?"

"Dr. Horz sells it at her veterinary office," I said. "But I haven't tried it. Rochester likes his food and he's healthy, so there's no reason to change."

"It seems a shame those people have come to such a beautiful setting, and they're stuck in meetings."

"Well, we're lucky not to be them."

Rochester pressed his nose between us, and Lili stroked his head.

Lili wanted to do some more sightseeing, so we got back in the car and left Centerbury behind for a countryside of rolling hills and farms. The area was a riot of color, from the stark white of country churches to the dark red of barns and the green, gold and orange of trees. Lili took photos of trees and waterfalls and small children and she was as happy as I'd ever seen her.

By the time we returned to Centerbury, Lili had taken a lot of photos and Rochester and I had walked for miles.

We stopped for dinner at Olives and Feta to use the coupon we'd received, and I was pleased to see a sign proclaiming, "Well-behaved dogs are always welcome."

"That sounds like you, Rochester," I said, as we parked.

The same woman who'd given us the coupon greeted us at the

door in a blue and white dress, the colors of the Greek flag. "I'm Sue Flocky," she said. "Welcome to Olives and Feta."

Rochester sniffed her shoes, a pair of dark blue restaurant clogs that resembled Crocs, and then stepped back. Probably didn't like whatever she'd stepped in.

"Oh, I recognize you," she said. "Didn't I speak to you yesterday?"

"You did," I said.

"Well, I'm delighted you decided to join us. I'm your host, and my husband Aristotle is in the kitchen." She took us to a table by the window, and Rochester settled alongside the wall, without paying any attention to Sue.

"Can I offer you some ouzo to prepare your taste buds and open your appetites?" she asked, as she handed us our menus.

We agreed, and after the drinks we shared a platter of stuffed grape leaves and spanakopita, a mix of flaky pastry and creamy spinach. I ordered the moussaka and Lili the lamb stew. We'd brought Rochester's bowl and chow with us, and Lili dropped bits of lamb into it for him.

Sue came by with our entrées. "Are you staying here in town?"

"At the Otter Creek Inn," Lili said.

Sue's face darkened. "Are you part of Dr. M's crew?"

Lili shook her head. "No, one of the rooms opened up at the last minute."

"How did you know that his family were staying there?" I asked. "Are you a fan of his dog foods?"

"Not at all. I wouldn't feed that crap to anyone or their dog. But the small businesses here in Centerbury share information. I recommend people to the inn, and Ophelia sends guests here."

She returned to the kitchen. The food was delicious, and we couldn't resist sharing a plate of baklava for dessert. We didn't get back to the Otter Creek Inn until almost eight o'clock. Dr. M and his son were arguing again in the lobby as we walked in. "I'm glad we got away from here for a while," Lili whispered to me.

It seemed to be a rehash of the same argument Dr. M had mentioned to me the night before. "I can't keep going over this again and again," Dr. M said. "I'm so tired. I can barely consider walking Janie."

The white-faced golden was on the floor beside him. She looked old and tired, and I wondered if Dr. M's exhaustion had led to the petition Rochester had found earlier that day.

"Dad. You shouldn't have brought the dog with you if you can't take care of her."

"Janie is the only one in this family who gives me unconditional love."

"Fine. I'll take her. Let me borrow your coat."

Dr. M frowned. "I really should go out with her, but I need to rest. My coat is right over there on the sofa."

Alistair walked over to the sofa and grabbed the camel hair trenchcoat. He returned to his father, who handed him the dog's leash, and he stalked out, nearly dragging the old dog behind him.

"I should take Rochester while we're up and dressed," I said. We went outside, but I went in the opposite direction of Alistair and his father's dog.

Rochester and I circled around, up and down a hill, and then walked back toward the inn. On the way I spotted Janie, on her own and trailing her leash behind her.

"Honestly. Some people," I grumbled. Rochester tugged me toward her.

I leaned down and grabbed her leash. "Where's your human?" I asked. Had Alistair abandoned the dog and gone back to the inn?

She turned around and walked slowly back in the direction she'd come from. Rochester and I followed.

We saw a man sitting on a bench, bent over and looking at his cell phone in his hand. He wore a camel hair coat and had light-colored hair, and I thought it had to be Dr. M's son Alistair.

"Hello?" I called. "Isn't this your father's dog?"

He didn't respond. As we got closer, I realized that Alistair wasn't bent over, he was slumped down. "Oh, Jesus," I said. Had he had a heart attack? He was young for a stroke. One of my fears was that I'd be walking Rochester and something would happen to me that would leave him on his own.

We got up close to him, and I noticed a trail of blood coming from the back of his neck, exposed from the collar of his father's coat.

This wasn't a heart attack.

I couldn't help myself. I shone the flashlight from my phone on the wound. It was a small dark circle, with a round pattern of tiny dots around it, like deadly freckles.

I pulled my phone back, turned off the flashlight, and dialed 911. "I'm a tourist in town, so I'm not sure where I am," I said, when the operator answered. "But I found a man and he's bleeding."

"Can he tell you where you are?"

"I don't think he's still alive. It looks like he has a bullet hole in the back of his neck. But I don't want to touch him. Can't you use my phone's location?"

"Our system doesn't work well with cell phones," she said. "You say you're in town. Do you mean Centerbury?"

"Yes. I'm staying at the Otter Creek Inn. That's up the hill from here a couple of blocks."

"Good," she said. "I'm dispatching emergency services and I'll tell them a more exact location as we figure it out. Stay on the line, please."

She was gone for a moment or two, then back. "Tell me what you see around you. Any businesses?"

I looked around. "There's a beauty parlor across the street. Curl Up and Dye."

"That's good. That's where I get my hair cut, so I know the location. You're across the street?"

"I am. The man is on a park bench."

"Okay. Stay on the line while I relay that information."

She was back again. "Without touching him, can you see any evidence that he's breathing? Is his body moving at all?"

I shook my head, then realized she couldn't see me. "No. And it's really cold here."

I was shivering despite my coat, gloves, scarf, and hat. Probably shock. I heard a distant siren. "I hear someone coming," I said.

"Just stay right there. You're doing very well."

"He had a dog with him, and I have mine. I don't want to keep them out in the cold too long."

"I understand. But dogs are resilient. And if you can hear the siren, the EMTs will be with you soon."

The dispatcher was right; only a couple of minutes later the red and blue lights of a police car lit up the area. It pulled up in front of where Alistair Mihaly sat and two officers jumped out. One of them went up to Alistair and the other came over to me.

I explained to him what had happened, and by the time I finished a fire rescue truck had arrived. I told the officer who I thought the dead man was, and gave him my name and phone number. I said I was staying at the Otter Creek Inn, and he let me and Rochester and Janie head back.

Chapter 10
The Young Detective

I was thoroughly chilled by the time I got back to the inn, and Rochester and I stopped at the fireplace to warm up. I looked around for someone from the company to tell them about Alistair and spotted his sister. She wore a puffy down coat and fur-lined Crocs, and Ming Chow, now clean and fluffy, poked his head out of the top of her shoulder bag.

I walked up to her with both dogs. "What are you doing with Janie?" she asked.

Her tone was irritated more than questioning. As if I'd stolen her father's dog.

Dr. M's golden wasn't that eager to go over to her. Maybe she had already bonded with Rochester.

I handed her the leash. "I have some bad news for you. Janie was running loose and when I got hold of her she led me back to your brother. I'm afraid he was shot."

Her mouth gaped open. "Alistair?"

I nodded. "I'm very sorry. I called the police. I'm sure someone will be here to speak to you."

"I have to talk to my father." She tugged on Janie's leash. "Come on, let's go see Daddy."

Janie followed her, with one look back at Rochester.

I wondered why Rochester didn't seem to like Zoe Mihaly. Usually he loved anyone who appreciated dogs. Was it that he didn't like Ming Chow, the Bichon? Or was there something about Zoe that triggered him?

My dog and I warmed up by the fire for a few minutes. I wondered how soon the police would arrive, and if I'd made a mistake telling Zoe about her brother. I knew that Rick liked to observe suspects when he passed on bad news.

Beverly had mentioned there was bad blood in the family and the business, and Zoe had been wearing her coat when I found her. That meant either she'd been outside with Ming Chow or was about to go out. If she'd been outdoors when her brother was shot, that made her a prime suspect.

When the chill had left my face and hands, Rochester and I went back to the room. "You were gone for a while," Lili said. "Was Rochester giving you trouble?"

I sat down on the bed and sighed. "He did it again."

"What? Had diarrhea?"

I shook my head. "Found another dead body."

"Steve. We can't leave that behind for a week? It's like bodies follow you wherever you go."

"Don't look at me. Look at the dog."

She looked at me. "Who was it?"

"Alistair Mihaly. Doctor M's son."

"I don't suppose there's a chance it was natural causes?"

"Not with a bullet hole in the back of his neck."

"Well, at least Rick isn't involved, so he can't rope you in. We're just a pair of innocent tourists on our honeymoon."

"That's true."

She put her hand on mine. "You're still cold. Let's get under the covers so you can warm up."

We did, but as we drifted off to sleep I kept seeing that pattern of deadly freckles.

Food of the Dogs

I was getting ready to take Rochester out the next morning when the phone in our room rang. "This is Ophelia from the front desk. May I speak with Mr. Levitan?"

"That's me."

"There's a police detective here who would like to speak with you. Do you want me to send him to your room?"

"Can I meet him in the lobby?"

"I'll tell him."

I hung up and turned to Lili. "Can you take Rochester out while I talk to the detective?"

"Make it quick. I have more leaf-peeping on my agenda today."

The man waiting for me in the lobby looked young enough to be an Eastern College student. "Mr. Levitan? I'm Detective Pete Ecker. Thanks for talking with me."

We shook hands. "Mind if I get some coffee?" I asked.

"No problem." As we walked over to the breakfast display, Lili and Rochester came into the lobby behind us. They went to the front door, and I poured a coffee for myself.

"Can I pour you one?" I asked.

"I probably shouldn't. That's for guests."

"I'm sure the management won't mind," I said. I dispensed a cup for him and he put his own cream and sugar into it, and we walked over to a pair of chairs by the window.

"I hope you'll forgive me if I'm a bit uncertain," he said. "The regular detective in charge of this kind of investigation is on maternity leave. This is my first homicide, though I've been at plenty of crime scenes as an officer. I have a bachelor's in criminal justice and I went through the certification courses from the Vermont Police Academy, and I watch a ton of those CSI programs on TV." He smiled. "It's way different in a small town, and I'm struggling to put all my book learning into practice."

"No problem. My best friend back home is a homicide detective, so I know the drill." I told him what I'd witnessed the night before, starting with Alistair and his father arguing.

"He and Janie, that's the dog, went to the right, and Rochester and I went to the left. It was only when we were circling back toward the inn that I saw Janie loose, her leash dragging behind her."

Ecker sipped his coffee. "You were already familiar with the dog?"

"Dr. M and I discussed our goldens, and the connection between their names." He looked confused. "Rochester and Jane are both characters in the novel *Jane Eyre*, by Charlotte Bronte. Though I don't think that matters to your investigation."

He wrote that down anyway.

"What did you do after you saw the dog?"

"Rochester wanted to play with her, so he tugged me towards her. She turned around and walked back to where Mr. Mihaly was on the bench. I spoke to him and when he didn't respond I came up closer. That's when I realized he hadn't just fallen asleep. I saw the blood on the back of his neck and I called 911."

"You didn't try to revive him?" Ecker took another sip of his coffee, and I did, too. It was good, and I wondered what kind of beans they used. I might suggest them to Gail Dukowski, who ran the Chocolate Ear café where Rick and I regularly met.

I shook my head. "It looked like a crime scene to me and I didn't want to disturb anything."

"That was probably a good idea," he said. "You didn't see anyone else in the area?"

"No. I heard a few cars go by on other streets, but Rochester and I were on our own."

Two women came into the lobby then and walked toward the coffee and pastries. I recognized Beverly, the woman we'd spoken with the morning before.

"I have something to give you," I said. I pulled out the crumpled piece of paper Rochester had found near Alistair's body. "My dog found this on the street near where Alistair was killed. It looks like he was trying to have his father declared incompetent. Maybe so that he could take over the company."

Ecker looked at it. "I've never seen a form like this, but my experience has been limited. I'll have to check with my chief and see if he knows about this kind of thing."

"I know that Alistair and his father were arguing over the future of the company. I think you'll find if you talk to the other people staying here that there was tension between them, and maybe between other people, too."

"I've already spoken with Dr. Mihaly, Ms. Zoe Mihaly, and Mr. Winston Mihaly," he said. "None of them mentioned any tension within the family. But I have the names of all the other family and board members on my list, and I'll be sure to ask them. If anything comes up I can go back to the Mihalys for more information."

"Were you able to collect any evidence from the scene last night?" I asked.

"I can't say," he said. "Police business, you know."

Ecker drained the rest of his coffee, then stood up. "Thank you, Mr. Levitan." He pulled a business card from his wallet and handed it to me. "If you think of anything else, please let me know."

I looked at his card. "Your email address is pecker@Centerburypolice.gov?"

He looked chagrined. "I know. It's unfortunate the way they use the first initial and last name."

"Well, at least your name isn't Sam Hit," I said. "Good luck with your investigation."

He shook my hand again. "Thank you. And I'll keep Mr. Hit in mind when I worry about my email address."

Lili and Rochester came back in, and she joined me at the pastry table for tiny chocolate chip muffins and another cup of coffee. I fed Rochester bits of croissant as I told Lili about the detective. "He looks like a college kid," I said. "But he has to be older. Rick had to be on patrol for a couple of years before he qualified as a detective."

"He said he's the only detective?"

"I got the feeling it was an interim thing, while the regular detective is on maternity leave."

She looked at me. "I see the look in your eyes, Mr. Levitan. You want to get involved."

I played innocent. "I'm just a tourist on my honeymoon."

"Yet you brought your hacker laptop with us."

"In case Rick needed anything while I was away."

She shook her head. "I don't know what I'm going to do with you." She drained her coffee. "Let's hit the road."

Chapter 11
Footprint

"Do you mind if we go back past the park bench where I found the body last night?" I asked. "I want to look around."

"You think you'll find something the police didn't?"

"Rochester might. You know his record at sniffing out clues. And there's no dedicated crime scene team here, just a bunch of patrol officers. I asked Ecker if there was any evidence around the bench, but he wouldn't say. Which might be police protocol, or might mean he didn't find anything."

"Fine. But I want to get on the road soon."

It was a gorgeous, sunny day, and it was a pleasure to be out in the crisp air, surrounded by trees coming into their fall colors. We walked down the hill and around the corner to where I'd seen Alistair Mihaly. Crime scene tape was wrapped around the bench.

Rochester and I walked in a circuit around the bench, and he had his nose to the ground, sniffing. He probably smelled Janie—she'd been there the night before and might have left her mark. I knew that both males and females did that.

He tugged me away, in the direction toward where we'd found Janie, and then he stopped and pawed the ground. He lifted his front paw to move a fern leaf, and beneath it I saw what looked like a footprint. "Lili, can you come over here?" I called.

"What did you find?" she asked as she joined us.

"Looks like a footprint. But it's back from the bench so the police might not have seen it. Can you take a picture of it? Then maybe we can match it to the kind of shoe. It might help Detective Ecker narrow down his suspects."

She took several shots from different angles. Then I cut off some of the loose crime scene tape and used several twigs to set off the area. I had Lili take another picture then and send it to me, and I forwarded it to the detective.

"Our work here is done," I said. "Where do you want to go?"

"Today I want to head south," Lili announced as we walked back to the inn. "Southeast, actually. You'll be pleased to know there's a town called Rochester."

"Really?" I leaned down and scratched my dog under his chin. "A whole town named after you, boy."

"Supposedly some good leaf color there. And from there I want to head to Rutland. How about if we make a deal? I'll leave you and the hound at a café with wi-fi access while I wander around the town taking pictures?"

"You're too good to me," I said, and I kissed her cheek. "And you know me all too well."

"I wouldn't have married you if I didn't," she said.

There wasn't much to the town of Rochester, but Lili did take a very cute photo of the dog posed in front of the town sign. That immediately went up on my Facebook page.

Detective Ecker called as we were getting back in the car. "Thanks for the picture you sent," he said. "I went out there and took a cast of the footprint. How did you notice that? It was nearly hidden by the ferns."

"My dog found it," I said. "He has a knack for that kind of thing."

"Maybe I should get a dog, then," Ecker said. "I keep losing my house keys."

Food of the Dogs

"Rochester's special," I said, though I didn't go into details of all the clues he'd found over the years.

We stopped several times on Route 7 so Lili could take pictures, but she wasn't as excited by the landscape as she'd been. I started to worry that Lili was losing her enthusiasm, and wonder if we could get out of our commitment to the inn and head home earlier.

On the other hand, I wanted to stick around to see what Pete Ecker came up with. Because Rochester and I had found Alistair Mihaly's body, I had a personal stake in the case. And I wasn't sure Pete, as a novice, could manage without some discreet help.

We got to Rutland late in the morning. I parked on one side of a triangular-shaped brick building that housed an art gallery, and Lili said, "I'm going to walk around for a while. Why don't you settle into that café over there and I'll find you when I'm finished."

"Mountain Brews it is," I said. She walked off, and Rochester and I did a brief meander before settling in at the café. I ordered a decaf café mocha, careful to keep my caffeination within reasonable limits, and while Rochester munched on a sugar-free peanut butter muffin, I set up my hacker laptop.

I wasn't the only one trying to get some work done. All around me people were plugged in, often with headphones. Some were in their teens or twenties, with the wild haircuts college students often experiment with—dreads, high and tight fades, and colors in shades of blue and purple. A few were middle-aged working folks in suits or other formal clothes, tele-commuting or checking their emails. Then there were the elderly, women in gray braids and men who were mostly bald but with tiny pigtails at their backs. They wore the most colorful clothing, from tie-dyed T-shirts to flowing dresses in rainbow colors.

It made me feel at home, as I caught glimpses of games and spreadsheets and documents. But I wanted to be careful, so the first thing I did was enable my VPN; I didn't want anyone to be able to see what I was doing.

I decided to indulge my curiosity about the Mihaly family first, beginning with Alistair, the victim. But how? I stared at my screen and several of the icons at the bottom caught my eye. Of course, I was working on my hacker laptop. Why not let my fingers go running on the dark web and see what I could come up with?

Detective Ecker probably didn't have the skills I did at his disposal. If I found anything useful, I could figure out a way to pass it on to him that didn't incriminate me.

That was all I needed. I opened an online program and input all the names I had, then set it loose. I usually kept the machine turned on while I was running that kind of search, but because all the work was being done on a remote server, it would display the results the next time I logged in.

Results began to come in, and I began with Alistair. Piecing together information from LinkedIn as well as other sites, I found that he had grown up in Centerbury and attended the college there, where he'd majored in economics.

I was surprised to learn that he had a criminal record. He and another Centerbury student, Robert Hines, had been arrested for stealing drugs from Dr. M's veterinary clinic and selling them to classmates. Alistair had been convicted and given a suspended sentence of one year. During that time he was obliged to avoid committing future crimes and complete a thousand hours of community service.

An article from the *Daily Crier*, the Centerbury newspaper, spelled things out further. He had been put on a semester's academic probation from the College. Rather than sit around his parents' house, he chose to travel to Hungary for that term to volunteer as a veterinary technician in a clinic owned by a distant relative. That covered his thousand hours.

When he returned, he finished his degree, and he'd managed to keep his nose clean since then. Or at least my search program couldn't find any other arrests.

Hines had not been treated so well. He had been expelled from Centerbury and sentenced to two years at Northwest State Correctional Facility. I immediately set up a search for more information on him. If he was still in Centerbury he might have a big grudge against Alistair.

After graduation, Alistair moved to Manhattan where he worked in banking for a decade, beginning as an assistant manager at a branch near Wall Street and eventually becoming a loan officer and then branch manager. As he moved up the ranks, he pursued an MBA degree part-time.

One of his banking clients was a small start-up company that ran a website where people could resell their fashionable clothes. After receiving his MBA, he joined them as VP of finance and guided them through an initial public offering.

A few years later he shifted to a similar start-up focused on fast fashion. Their designers went to all the big fashion shows and picked items they thought could sell well. Then they crafted knockoffs which were manufactured in Vietnam and Malaysia. The company went public and he cashed out. His last listed job was as president of Dr. M's Healthy Dog Foods, Inc.

I remembered my conversation with Dr. M, who was worried that Alistair would try and build the company by sending production overseas. A reasonable worry, given his son's work history.

I found a photo of him and his wife at a charity affair, and recognized her as the woman he'd been talking with at breakfast. She was tall and slim, in a blood-red dress so unusual that it had to be a designer original. It began at her left shoulder and sloped down below her right breast, though a large white flower covered that. It had a matching white belt and a long skirt with a slit up the side. She had posed for the photo with her long, shapely right leg exposed.

She looked like a trophy wife, but she was about the same age as her husband. I wondered if she'd be able to pursue what was apparently an expensive lifestyle if her husband was dead and his income shut off. Dr. M's was still a relatively small business, privately held, with annual revenues of about $5 million.

One of my hacker programs let me snoop into its capitalization table, a spreadsheet that showed who had invested in the company, including common stock shares, preferred stock shares, warrants, and convertible equity. Dr. M owned fifty-one percent of the company, and each of his three children owned fifteen percent. The rest was owned by a pair of venture capital firms that had funded his startup.

I did some more searching and found that Alistair's salary in the previous year had been $250,000 as well as a performance bonus allowing him to buy shares of unissued stock at below-market price. Those were shares that were authorized for use in the company's charter but that the company had not yet sold.

The condo on Manhattan's Upper West Side where they lived was registered in his name only. It was valued at over $5 million, with a mortgage of nearly that much. Taxes and condo fees were high. Reading between the lines, it was clear that he was borrowing against his expectations. If he didn't get a raise soon, or take over the company and his father's ownership, he was facing a serious cash problem.

He and Katherine had married five years before. She had a degree in cosmetics and fragrance marketing from the Fashion Institute of Technology, and had been a fashion model before her marriage, mostly catalog work. She was involved in numerous charities, including mentoring single mothers and reading to children at low-achieving schools. She was photographed at many fund-raising events, where reference was often made to the designers who fashioned her clothes.

They had no children. A year before, Katherine had joined the board of Dr. M's Healthy Dog Foods. Each of the members was paid $60,000 a year plus expenses to attend board meetings.

I sat back. Sixty grand seemed like a lot of money, but when I did a quick comparison search I found it was reasonable for a profitable small company.

I didn't envy Detective Ecker having to talk to her about her husband and his death. The wife is always an early suspect in any

Food of the Dogs

homicide, and from the icy stare in her picture I thought she'd be a tough person to interview.

It didn't appear that she'd ever used her degree for anything, though it was possible she consulted with her husband on marketing. Which might have caused some friction with her sister-in-law, since that was Zoe's job, as vice president for marketing.

Zoe had a more checkered background. She had spent her freshman year at Goucher College in Maryland, then spent the summer in an expensive drug rehab facility in California. She attended a community college in Wisconsin for a couple of terms, then bounced back to rehab.

Eventually she finished a bachelor's degree in marketing at Long Island University, and then held several low-level jobs in marketing before being named VP at her father's company. She was single, and did no charitable work, but she had an active social media profile, often featuring her Bichon, Ming Chow.

If Zoe was a dog lover, why had Janie been reluctant to go with her? Because Janie didn't get along with Ming Chow? Back at River Bend, many little dogs barked and growled at Rochester, which I took to be a Napoleon complex. Perhaps the same was true between these two.

There was clearly bad blood between Zoe and both her brothers. But could she have gone after him and shot him in the back of the head? She didn't seem like the kind of Type A personality who would do anything to gain control of the family business. But did she have a long-lasting grudge that had bubbled up to the surface when the family was isolated together in Centerbury?

From Alistair and Zoe I jumped to information on the company. I recognized Beverly, the corporate secretary. Kelsey Morrison was the treasurer. The board of directors included Dr. M, Alistair, Zoe, and three outside members.

I closed my eyes and tried to remember our conversation with Beverly. One of the directors had gotten sick at the last minute and cancelled, opening his room to us. What was his name? I looked at the list and made the connection. Frank Payne was the man who'd gotten sick.

I wondered why Winston Mihaly wasn't a director of the company, and why he was in Centerbury. Was Dr. M trying to draw him in? Or was he there to get money from his father? A quick search on his name showed that he had won a few ski races in Colorado over the past few years, and that he taught skiing at an exclusive school in Breckenridge. He didn't own real estate, which meant he was living in rented places.

He had a Facebook page, but for the most part all he did was post profile pictures and the occasional photo of a race or a winning prize. He was mentioned by others periodically, usually at fancy parties where he was often photographed with a shot glass in his hand.

Could he have killed his older brother? Out of jealousy? Some childhood anger that had been percolating? Did he want to take over Alistair's position as favorite son? It was always fascinating to me that the more you dug into someone's life, the more ugly secrets you could find.

Sadly, one of those had probably gotten Alistair Mihaly killed.

Chapter 12
Framing

Lili joined us at the café, and we ate sandwiches on homemade bread. Hers had honey turkey, mine roast beef, and both were delicious, accompanied by a local brand of hand-made potato chips and bottles of Rugged Mountain Root Beer, brewed close by.

"Did you find anything interesting?" Lili asked as we ate.

I told her what I'd dug up about the family and their background in Centerbury. She was intrigued by the way that like me, Alistair had bounced back from criminal charges.

"Do you think someone local might be responsible for Alistair's death?" she asked. "Even if that boy he was convicted with is out of the picture, there might be someone else holding a grudge."

"I'm just gathering data right now. But any time you have a history in a place, there can be old problems waiting to percolate up to the top. Remember that sneaker Rochester found at the Friends' Meeting House? How many old resentments came up when I started snooping into the people who opposed the Vietnam conflict?"

"Including an old man with a shotgun."

"Let's not consider him." The thought reminded me of all those people who might have a grudge against me back in Stewart's Crossing, because of work I'd done to help Rick put people behind bars.

"The whole small-town thing is still new to me," she said. "Even after four years in Stewart's Crossing. I'm accustomed to life in the big city where you don't even know the people in the apartment next to yours."

"Sometimes that's better," I said.

We took a long stroll through the town on our way back to the car. Rutland was like Centerbury in many ways. A sloping Main Street, small shops and restaurants, and a quaint, New England feel. We passed a ski shop with a bunch of metal stands out front holding local penny savers and free magazines geared to skiers. Rochester was particularly interested in one, and I had to tug him away before he peed against it.

As I did, I noticed the headline on the front page of the paper, a local one called *South Vermont News*. "Brattleboro Nursing Scandal." That must have been the case Rick had mentioned before we left Stewart's Crossing. I picked up a copy and tucked it into my messenger bag.

We crossed the street then and walked through a small park, and Rochester assumed the poop position. I grabbed a grocery bag from my pocket and picked up after him, and then found a waste can on our way back to the car.

We drove a circular route back to Centerbury. Lili had to be at the college at three-thirty for her lecture to Eva Alvarez's class, but we had enough time to stop at a scenic overlook. Though Lili got out of the car and looked through her viewfinder several times, by the time she'd gotten back in the car she'd only taken one photo.

"Maybe I burned myself out in Rutland, but I'm more interested in pulling the pictures I've already taken into Photoshop and playing with them. Sometimes the most interesting thing about a picture is how you frame it, and I can do a lot to crop and refocus using tools. Tomorrow we'll stay in Centerbury and I'll see what there is to shoot in the town, and spend some time on my computer."

"Works for me," I said. "I'm getting tired of driving, and we have a long haul back to Pennsylvania on Sunday."

We drove for a while, and then I asked, "What was your favorite part of the wedding?"

"I already know what yours was," Lili said. "Rochester slipping away from Joey and Mark and rushing down the aisle toward you."

"That was pretty special," I said. "But not my favorite part."

"Really? Then what was?"

"Seeing your face when you walked into the synagogue and spotted me in the morning coat. I wanted to do everything I could to make the wedding special for you, and I knew that was one of your dreams."

"I did love that," she said. "It spoke volumes. That you heard that, and remembered it, and did it for me. All my wedding jitters were gone by then, but if I still had some, they would have disappeared."

She reached over and patted my leg, and Rochester stuck his head between the seats to see what was going on.

Then Lili looked out the window, thinking. I waited to hear what her favorite part of the wedding was.

"Would you be upset if I told you my favorite part wasn't about you?" she asked when she looked back at me.

I shrugged. "Not particularly."

"It was having all my family around me," she said. "I hadn't realized how much I missed that."

"Saul told me that his daughter Talia is getting married in San Salvador in the spring," I said.

"When did you talk to Saul?"

"At the reception. He was impressed that we pulled everything together so quickly. That his wife and Talia have been obsessing for months."

"I heard that, too."

"I want to take you there," I said. "To San Salvador, for the wedding."

She smiled. "Really? Another event full of my crazy relatives?"

"I thought they were all very nice. Even the poet with the tattoo and his angry father. Do you want to go?"

She leaned over and kissed my cheek. "Of course I do. I haven't been to El Salvador in ages. And I'm sure all my cousins will be there, too."

We arrived back in Centerbury in plenty of time to accompany Lili to Eva Alvarez's class. We parked at the Inn's lot, and I slung the messenger bag carrying my hacker laptop over my shoulder. Lili grabbed her camera and her bag of lenses, and we waited while Rochester announced to the world (and a potted chrysanthemum) that he was back in town.

When we walked inside we found Dr. M and most of his group in the lobby. As Lili walked to the room, Dr. M left a conversation with his son Winston and came over to me. His face was drawn and it looked like he hadn't slept.

"I understand you found Janie," he said. "Thank you for bringing her back safely."

I noticed he didn't say anything about his son, which was curious. "It wasn't a problem," I said. "Janie's a sweetheart. I'm very sorry about Alistair."

"My son and I had a difficult relationship," he said. "I'm sorry that the last words I had with him were angry ones."

"I was reading your company website and I saw that you used to practice here in Centerbury." Though I already knew about his family background, I didn't want to reveal to the good doctor that I'd been snooping. "Did Alistair grow up here?" I asked.

"He did. Went to the College as well."

"Do you think he ran into someone he knew? Someone who had a grudge against him?"

Dr. M hesitated, and I worried that I'd gone too far.

"He had a prickly personality," the doctor finally said. "He resisted coming back to Centerbury for this event because he worried that he'd run into old enemies. I told him he was being foolish." His shoulders sagged. "Perhaps I was wrong."

Food of the Dogs

Zoe came up then and put her arm through her father's. "We need to finish the meeting," she said. "All that time we took with the police has cut into our agenda."

I thought that was cold, but then, Dr. M said Alistair was prickly, and perhaps he didn't get along with his sister either.

"Thank you again," Dr. M said, and he walked off with Zoe.

When I got back to the room, Lili was modeling a khaki vest that had more pockets than a standard pool table, in different sizes. It looked like you could use it instead of a carry-on bag. "What do you think about wearing this vest?" she asked. "I thought I'd demonstrate how to carry all my cameras and lenses."

The vest looked over-the-top to me, but I wasn't going to say anything negative. "I'm sure the students will be interested in that."

She'd already gotten permission for Rochester and me to come with her, and she loaded up various pockets while I played tug-a-rope with Rochester.

We followed Main Street into the center of town, then climbed another hill to get to the college. A set of gray limestone buildings, a Victorian Gothic chapel, and a series of more modern buildings grouped around quads.

We followed a path to an older building called Founders' Hall, where Professor Alvarez held court in a light-flooded classroom.

She was a small, sprightly woman with a long gray braid. She wore a colorful Mexican serape over black slacks and welcomed Lili with a hug and kisses to both cheeks. "One of my best students at NYU," she said to her class, as part of her introduction.

I sat at the end of a long table at the back of the room with Rochester at my feet. Lilli had brought her presentation on a jump drive, and she lowered the lights and began to show images she had taken in her career.

Though I'd seen many of Lili's photos over the years, I was surprised at the breadth and the vision they displayed when they were all put together. Many were scenes of war and devastation, from bombed-out buildings to grime-faced soldiers. Often they were contrasted by lush tropical backgrounds or brilliant sunny skies.

"This was taken in Northern Ireland, as protesters stormed government buildings and were driven back by tear gas, clubs, and live ammunition," she said. "I tried to stay to the sidelines, but they were always moving. Eventually I found shelter behind a barricade of burning rubber tires and wooden pallets."

She looked at the class. "That's important. You have to protect yourself, but at the same time you are there to capture the emotion of a scene as well as document what's happening. It's a balancing act, and fortunately I was successful most of the time."

She flipped to another slide, a closeup of a teenaged man, his faced streaked with tears. He held a rifle in his hand. "Sometimes that involves framing the image to tell a story. What do you see in this photo?" she asked.

A young woman raised her hand. "A fighter."

Another said, "A rebel."

A young man added "Anti-government insurgent."

Lili said, "Now here's another shot of the same young man, at the same time, but with a wider angle."

Now we could see a small, frightened girl, clutching the young man's lower leg. Her dress was muddy and torn and she was missing one shoe.

"What do you see now?" Lili asked.

"A boy protecting his sister," a girl said.

There was general agreement.

"Do you see how the interpretation of the image changes depending on how the image is framed or cropped?" she asked.

I was fascinated, and I saw the students were as well. As Lili continued to lecture, I thought about the way I had been framing Alistair Mihaly's death. By focusing on him and his family, was I missing the larger picture?

I leaned down and stroked the top of Rochester's head. He'd brought me to Alistair's body, summoned by Janie. Then he'd discovered the footprint behind the bench, and the crumpled document Alistair might have planned to use to take over the company.

I was eager to get back to my hacker laptop and see if my programs had been able to dig up new information online. It was Wednesday, and we'd be leaving Centerbury on Sunday. That gave me an extra incentive to keep digging.

Chapter 13
Abandonment

I had to wait to see what other results my hacker programs had turned up, because Eva had invited us to dinner with some of her students at a Mexican restaurant called Guacstar near the campus.

"The owners are from Chiapas, Eva says, and the food is authentic to the southern part of Mexico," Lili said as we followed Eva, who led her students like a tour guide. "I was there during the Zapatista uprising and I ate some great food, between moments of sheer terror."

"Would you ever want to go back to that kind of life?" I asked.

She shook her head. "I was young and reckless and determined to get the shots I wanted. I couldn't do that again. And the kind of work I did was also heartbreaking. I focused on the effects of conflict on the local people. Families who lost their houses, children whose parents were killed. I still feel passionately about innocent victims, but I'd rather do my part from afar."

Guacstar was small and lively, with tables full of young people who were probably college students. Lots of Centerbury sweatshirts and ball caps, many of those turned backwards. Pitchers of beer on the tables along with trays of chips and bowls of salsa. "That's ranchera music in the background," Lili said as we walked in. "I heard a lot of that when I was in Mexico." She held up her hand. "Here it comes."

The music was interrupted by a loud yell from the musicians. "They call that yell the *grito mexicano*," she said. "I can't tell you how many hours I spent in bars listening to it."

Eva led us to a small private room at the rear of the restaurant, where we could talk with the half-dozen students who had accompanied us. As the guest of honor, Lili was surrounded by students. Rochester and I settled at the end of the table, him on the floor by me. A young man with flowing blond hair sat beside me, with Rochester between us.

"Hey, I'm Rowan. Do you mind if I pet your dog?" he asked.

"Not at all. Rochester loves attention."

Rowan knew exactly what Rochester liked, beginning by scratching behind his ears. "Man, I wish I could have a dog," he said. "But I live in the dorm, and my dad's allergic so I can't have one at home, either."

"That's a shame."

"I was lucky when I was a kid. I grew up next door to a veterinarian's family here in Centerbury, and there was a constant parade of dogs and cats and all kinds of animals there."

"Doctor Mihaly?" I asked.

"Oh, yeah, you know him?" Rowan pulled a rubber scrunchie from his pocket and tied back his hair.

I explained that the doctor and his family were in Centerbury for a meeting.

"Cool. Is Win with them?"

I nodded. "You know him?"

"He was my babysitter for a few years when I was a kid and he was a teenager. I used to go next door to play with the animals, and he and I would feed and walk and bathe the animals." Rowan laughed. "Now I look back and it was a kind of Tom Sawyer thing, right?"

Eva ordered a pitcher of margaritas for the table, and the server brought big bowls of tortilla chips and salsa in varying degrees of heat.

"You mean Tom convincing his friends it was fun to paint the fence he was supposed to?" I asked Rowan, between sips of the tart margarita.

He smiled. "Exactly. Win was multi-tasking before it even became a term. Looking after me and getting me to do his chores for him at the same time."

"It sounds like you had fun," I said.

"I did. But I could tell it was a sad house, you know? Their mom was sick a lot, and then she went to a hospital. Doc was so involved with his patients and Alistair and Zoe were in college, and Win was left on his own. I think he was glad to hang out with me even though I was so much younger."

We ordered a couple of platters of nachos, and I ordered a grilled breast of chicken, which I shared with Rochester. Rowan turned to the young woman next to him, and I spoke to a different guy across the table. But I kept thinking about the Mihaly family after Mrs. Mihaly went to the hospital.

Was that experience why Alistair and Zoe had turned to drugs in college? A sense of loss and abandonment? That might be why Win hadn't settled down, too. I recalled that after he was suspended from Centerbury, Alistair had gone to Hungary for a semester. That might have added to Win's unhappiness and distance from his older brother.

But was there a motive for murder there, too? Of either Alistair or Doctor M?

Chapter 14
Healthy Foods

After we said goodbye to Eva and the students, we left Guacstar, the flavors of the food still with us. "We'll be able to eat like this in El Salvador," she said. "It's not that far from Oaxaca, just on the other side of Honduras. There are a lot of similarities between the cuisine."

"I'm looking forward to it," I said.

"I miss my cousins already," she said. I loved the way Lili lit up when she talked about seeing her family. "I got a ton of text messages. Everyone got home safely. But I think that's why I was a bit down today. Coming off the high of seeing them all."

"I guess my company can't make up for dozens of cousins."

She took my hand. "That's not what I meant. I didn't have a big wedding or a honeymoon with either Philip or Adriano, so I didn't know what to expect."

"My honeymoon with Mary was less than spectacular," I said. "I thought it was going to be the two of us, walking on the beach, kissing in the moonlight, that kind of thing. But she couldn't let things go—if the server at dinner was slow, it was like the whole meal was ruined for her. She probably spent half the time we were in Hawaii crying."

"That must have been terrible for you."

"I just wanted to make her happy," I said. "I made jokes, I sang her little songs. Don't get me wrong, we had some fun. But we were both glad to get back to our regular lives."

I squeezed her hand. "Fortunately I think things are going pretty well for us on this honeymoon. Aside from Alistair Mihaly's death."

"Aside from that," she said, and she kept my hand in hers as we walked back to the Inn.

It was still early in the evening, and after spending so much time among photography students, Lili wanted to transfer photos from her cameras to her computer and play around with them. I let her use the table in the room and took Rochester down the hill to a dog-friendly coffee shop called Cool Beans Café. I settled him at a table and ordered a decaf mocha, treating myself to an extra pump of raspberry syrup. It was about seven o'clock in the evening, and the café was humming.

Someone had left a copy of the Centerbury daily paper on one of the tables, and I noticed there was an article about Alistair's murder, though there was nothing there I didn't already know.

Once I had my coffee, I hooked up to their wi-fi, initiated my VPN software, and checked on the progress of my searches. I realized that if I wanted to think about Dr. M as the killer's intended target, I needed to know more about him, so I began with the results about him.

He was born in Brattleboro, just north of the Massachusetts border. He had gotten his undergraduate degree at the University of Vermont, and gone on to receive his DVM at Tufts. There were thirty-two colleges of veterinary medicine in the US, and if you didn't live in a state that had its own school you had to compete for a place in a neighboring state, one that had an agreement with your home. It made sense that he'd have gone from UVM to Massachusetts.

After graduation he secured an internship with Dr. Marvin Chappell, a vet in Centerbury, and eventually became a partner in the clinic. After ten years, Chappell had retired, and Dr. M had brought in a series of junior vets who each stayed for a few years.

Food of the Dogs

According to the company website, he had become interested in nutrition when his own golden retriever began having kidney problems, and he'd done a lot of research into dog foods. He had published his book on canine nutrition, the one I'd picked up at the used bookstore. Then he gradually scaled back his work to concentrate on his research.

Once he had launched Dr. M's Healthy Dog Foods, he turned the practice over to the current junior vet, Dr. Jason Evangelos, and moved to Wisconsin, where he opened a small factory and focused on the business.

In the past ten years, the factory had grown, becoming the largest employer in the county where it was located. The product line expanded to include puppy chow, specially formulated food for large breeds, and senior foods, as well as for kidney care and weight loss.

That was all I could find on him for the time being, so I returned to my search results. Beverly Thompson, the corporate secretary, had graduated from the University of Wisconsin with a BBA degree in business. She had been with Dr. M for a decade, beginning as his personal assistant when he launched the dog food company. She was unmarried, owned a home in Lakewood Hills, near Dr. M's lakefront home in Maple Bluff and the corporate headquarters near the Dane County airport.

She served on the board of the Wisconsin Humane Society, earned $80,000 a year, and owned ten percent of the company's stock. She seemed to be the consummate employee, devoting much of her life to the company and its goals, even in her spare time. Could she have come to resent those sacrifices? I'd only seen her be pleasant in public, so it was hard to think about a motive she might have to kill either Alistair or Doctor M. But I'd keep an open mind.

Henry Rozell was a board member, a pharmacist in Madison, and an adjunct professor at the university. He advised Dr. M about the chemical properties of additives used in the formulations of the different varieties of dog food. He was a member of the National

Rifle Association and in his youth had won several marksmanship medals.

I stared at the picture that accompanied his UW profile. I recognized him; he was the angry driver who'd nearly run into my car when he parked the day before.

He had a temper. What if he'd argued with Alistair over his plan to move production overseas? And say he'd brought a gun with him on the drive from Wisconsin, and stalked Alistair on Monday night? Or maybe he had a beef with Dr. M himself, and had mistaken Alistair for him?

There I went, spinning stories and coming up with suspects and motives, when it wasn't my business at all. I looked down at the dog. "I don't know what I'm doing," I said to him. "I'm just randomly collecting research."

He looked at me and began coughing. Had he swallowed something he found on the floor? I was about to pry open his jaws, but after a couple of coughs he was fine again.

"I hope you're not getting sick," I said to him. He looked up at me, then slumped back to the floor again.

Sick. Dr. Mihaly had mentioned he was in Brattleboro when something went wrong with his heart. Had he been in the hospital at the time of the nursing scandal? That was intriguing, so I closed the laptop and pulled out the newspaper to read about the case Rick had mentioned.

Hospital administration had noticed a series of problems in the cardiac care unit, where patients were administered the wrong drugs. It was unclear whether the mix-up occurred in supply rooms, with one drug being swapped for another, or whether nurses were administering the wrong drugs on their own. They had suspended all the nurses in the unit, replacing them with staff from other hospital departments.

Many hospitals had begun instituting computer systems that allowed nurses to scan patients' wrist bracelets with a handheld device, then scan the bar code on the pill bottle to make sure they matched. But Brattleboro Community was an older hospital and hadn't invested in those systems yet.

Several nurses were interviewed by the paper, and all of them professed their innocence. "Our nurses are all trained professionals, and while it's possible for one staff member to make a single mistake, the scale of this problem indicates something wrong," one of them said. "But to suspend all of us is too big a step."

A research professional had been interviewed about improper medications being given in hospitals and he stated, "An average of one medication error occurs per hospitalized patient per day. Many of them are in specialized units like CCUs. Patients who are conscious need to verify they are getting the right medication, and those who are unable to advocate for themselves need family or friends to do so."

I read further. One of the problems cited was that three elderly men with heart conditions had died in the CCU in close succession, and two others had recovered after near-death experiences. In all five cases, the men had suffered life-threatening arrhythmias.

Several common errors were mentioned. Calcium chloride could be given instead of calcium gluconate. They were two different kinds of calcium salts, used in different circumstances. Ajmaline was used to induce arrhythmic contractions when testing for a certain heart rhythm disorder, and it could be confused with accupril, used to treat heart failure.

The situation was still under review by the police and hospital administrators. I tore the article out to hand to Rick when I returned home, and then skimmed the rest of the paper. I'd finished my coffee long before, and I had some ideas but nothing concrete. Not that it was my business. I didn't know Alistair Mihaly or Detective Ecker, so I had no dog in the race. But it was fun to let my curiosity run when there was little at stake for me.

As Rochester and I walked back to the inn, we ran into Ethan, the clerk at the bookstore, and his basset hound. She was very lively, jumping and pulling on the leash in her desire to get close to Rochester.

We moved up so they could sniff each other, and immediately the basset rolled on her back.

"You are such a little slut, Daisy," Ethan said. Rochester sniffed her parts, and then she returned to her feet and they jumped around together.

"Let me guess," I said. "Daisy from *The Great Gatsby*?"

"Got it in one," Ethan said. "The curse of the English major. Everything we see reminds us of something in a book."

"I have that same curse, too," I said. "Though what I usually remember are puns and jokes."

Ethan said, "One of my classmates suggested that Jay Gatsby could open a florist that only sold one kind of flowers—daisies."

"What would you find in Charles Dickens' pantry?" I asked.

He put his lips together and thought for a moment, then his eyes lit up. "The best of thyme, and the worst of thyme."

We both laughed. Then Ethan said, "What kind of dinosaur writes novels?"

"Too easy. A Brontësaurus."

The dogs were still playing, so I asked, "Are you bringing Daisy to the opening of the dog park on Friday?"

"I'm not sure. The place has real bad memories for me."

"Really? What kind?"

"A friend of mine in college had a little Yorkshire Terrier he called Trotsky. Trotsky started to limp, and my friend took him into the vet's office that used to be there."

"Dr. M?" I asked.

"No, the young guy who took over from him. He thought Trotsky had a hernia, so he gave him anesthesia and started to operate. Couldn't find the hernia, though, so he kept looking, and by the time he gave up he couldn't revive Trotsky."

A cold wind picked up, swaying the branches of the oaks around us, and a few leaves fell to the ground. I tasted rain in the air. "That's a terrible shame."

"Oh, yeah, my friend was broken up about it. And that wasn't the first mistake that vet made."

"That's the one who ended up committing suicide?" I asked.

"Yeah. I don his name, but it was big news in town for a while."

Daisy finally had enough play with Rochester and tugged Ethan away, and we said goodnight. I had a new bride waiting for me at the Inn and I was eager to get back to her.

Chapter 15
Succession

When Rochester and I got back to the inn, Dr. M was sitting by the fire talking with Pete Ecker, with Janie by his side. Her tail began wagging when Rochester approached.

Though I wanted to get to the room, I also wanted to give my boy some play time. Lili could wait an extra few minutes. As we got closer, Ecker stood up and thanked Dr. M for his time, then walked over to a corner of the lobby and pulled out his phone. He had a newspaper under his arm, and I figured it was the same one I'd seen at the café.

Dr. M looked at Rochester, then up at me. "Many people think that dogs wag their tails because they're happy," he said. "But new research suggests that because humans respond to rhythm, they selected for that trait when breeding their first canine companions."

"That's interesting," I said, as Rochester went down into the play position in front of Janie. I sat on a wing chair across from the doctor.

"Rhythms — everything from music to the sound of pounding horse hoofs — trigger brain activity that helps make people feel joyful," Dr. M said. "If you watch their tails they even resemble a metronome."

"Seeing Rochester wag his tail does make me happy," I said. Dr. M and I watched the dogs play together for a few minutes.

"My daughter is keeping us focused on the business we need to finish while we're here," he said eventually. "It's more complicated now without Alistair. Sadly, she never got along with her brother, even when they were children. He was a smart boy and he got excellent grades while hardly trying. Zoe had to work harder for her grades, and she got angry when Alistair was playing instead of studying. I could bribe Alistair with computer games into helping at the clinic, but Zoe said it was too sad being around sick animals."

He sighed. "Alistair used to tease her sometimes. I remember I had to amputate the leg of a cocker spaniel once, and Alistair brought the dog into the house and made Zoe cry." He turned his head a bit to the side. "They were both my children but couldn't have been more different."

"What about Winston?" I asked.

"He was our youngest, and his mother and I used to joke that he had been left for us by elves. Always getting into mischief, the kind of boy who'd prefer to be outside swimming or skiing or playing sports when he was supposed to be working."

That connected with what Rowan had said to me at dinner, that Winston had tricked him into doing chores as if they were fun. And perhaps they were, if you loved the animals. I never minded grooming Rochester's hair, trimming his nails, brushing his teeth, or bathing him, because I loved him. It was sweet duty.

But other people's dogs and cats? Perhaps not.

"I'm faced with a difficult choice now," Dr. M said. "I had always intended that Alistair take over the business. Without him, I'm at a loss. Zoe is smart and she can grow into the job eventually, if her health holds up. Winston broke his leg skiing in the winter, and he said that has made him look more carefully at his future. He says he wants to get more involved in the business, but I'm not sure he has the temperament. I might end up having to look outside the family."

"Beverly, perhaps?"

He looked at me in surprise. "No, Beverly is a very good secretary and she does an excellent job of managing human resources. But I don't think she has the vision to run the whole company."

How did Beverly feel about that, I wondered. She'd devoted her life to Dr. M's Healthy Foods. If Alistair had taken over, would he have kept her?

Dr. M sighed, and then rose. With Janie trailing behind him, he walked toward the hallway leading to the rooms. I stood as well, but then Detective Ecker approached me. His brown hair was tousled and his face was drawn. It was after nine o'clock by then, so he was certainly working late.

"How are things going?" I asked.

"Pressure is heating up. We don't have many murders here in Centerbury, no more than two or three a year, and they're usually domestic. Couple argues, there's alcohol or drugs involved, and someone ends up dead. Cut and dried. This is different, though."

"I can imagine," I said. Stewart's Crossing and the surrounding township covered a lot more area than Centerbury, but the typical crimes were the same.

"I doesn't help that the newspaper has gotten hold of this," he said, holding up the copy. "There's only so many times I can say we're following leads before they start pestering the chief and then the mayor."

He sighed. "I don't mind admitting I'm kind of lost," he said. "I tried to sit down with the regular detective this afternoon and go through things, but her baby is very colicky and it was hard for her to concentrate. I don't have much experience on computers beyond video games, and the guys we rely on from the state police are backed up. I've got a lot of ideas but I'm struggling on how to carry them out."

"As I mentioned, my best friend is a homicide detective back home, and I help him out with computer research," I said. "I can do the same thing for you, if you'd like. I don't know any of these people or this town, so I might be able to give you a fresh perspective."

"That's a kind offer," he said. "But I'd have to check with chief first. We do bring in consultants now and then if we need their skills."

I pulled out my wallet. I always carried one of Rick's cards there. "Why don't you call my friend Rick and ask him what he thinks of me? That might reassure you and your chief."

He took the card. "Thanks."

"I hope he'll say good things," I said. "He was my best man at our wedding on Sunday. So he probably has a positive impression of me, at least for the moment."

Ecker laughed. "My friends run hot and cold on me sometimes, especially if I'm caught up in police stuff and drop out of meetups."

"Rick will tell you I'm congenitally curious," I said. "Discovering Alistair's body gives me a personal connection so I did some searching this afternoon."

So I jumped in with that I'd learned that afternoon about Alistair. "Did you know that Alistair was arrested here in Centerbury when he was a student at the college?"

He nodded. "His record came up in our system. But that was a long time ago."

"I know. But he was arrested with another student, Robert Hines, who got a much longer sentence than Alistair did. Do you know if Hines is still around? He's someone who might have a grudge against Alistair. And a motive for murder."

"I saw Hines was a co-defendant, but I didn't compare their sentences. You found that out online?"

"It was in a newspaper article. Alistair got suspended from the College for a semester, which he spent in Europe. Hines was sentenced to two years in prison, though I don't know how long he spent there."

He wrote "Hines?" in his notebook. "You think you could find more information like this?"

"I know I can. And Rick will probably tell you that Rochester here has a nose for clues. He's the one who found that footprint, and the piece of paper I gave you."

I figured since we were on good terms I could press him. "Did you look into that? If Alistair wanted to have his father declared incompetent, that would give Dr. M a motive to kill him."

"As far as I can tell the motion was never filed," Ecker said. "But Dr. M might have known about it. It's a big stretch for a father to kill a child, though. You've talked to Dr. M, haven't you?"

"I have."

"Does he seem to be that kind of cold-blooded person? Determined to keep control of his company at all costs?"

"I haven't seen that in him," I admitted. "Though I've only had a couple of casual conversations with him, usually about dogs. But he did tell me that he wanted Alistair to succeed him, though on his own terms, not Alistair's. He sounds very passionate when he talks about the company's products and the effect they can have on dogs' lives."

"It's confusing," Ecker said. "But then, human beings can maintain opposing points of view in their brains. Just look at politics. People hate a candidate for one thing but love him for another."

By then, I'd begun to feel more reassured about Pete Ecker's capabilities. He was doing all the things that Rick would have been doing—interviewing suspects, reviewing evidence, talking to witnesses. But I was sure he could benefit from some discreet help.

He slipped Rick's card into his pocket. "I'll call your friend. If the chief agrees, I'll be in touch."

He left, and Rochester and I went back to the room. "I did some fiddling with the photo I took of that footprint," Lili said, as I poured chow into a bowl for the hound. "I enlarged it and made the edges crisper, and then I uploaded it to Google's image search."

"You're getting to be a detective yourself," I said.

"It's all your influence," she said. "It matches the sole of a Croc. They're unisex shoes, so I can't tell if it belonged to a woman or a man. It's a smaller size, probably the eight-inch, which makes it more like that it belongs to a woman."

"I saw Zoe Mihaly wearing fur-lined Crocs last night," I said. "But I didn't measure her feet."

"That's probably a good thing." She yawned. "Ready for bed? Or for enjoying our honeymoon?"

I smiled. "I can get behind that idea."

Chapter 16
Rainy Day

Thursday morning dawned significantly colder. It had rained during the night, and many of the trees around us had lost their leaves before they'd had the chance to change color.

Rochester went to the French doors that led from our room to the inn's garden. So I followed his lead, and instead of going through the lobby, I slid the doors open.

"I noticed something when I was looking for Ming Chow," I said. "Several of the other rooms on the first floor have French doors. Anyone in a room like ours could have gotten outside the night of Alistair's murder without passing through the lobby. I'll have to mention that to Pete Ecker."

"Your new best friend," Lili said. "Rick will be jealous."

"I'm sure Rick has his hands full back home," I said.

I hurried Rochester through his business, and stopped in the lobby to pick up breakfast for Lili and me. Beverly Johnson was sitting by herself in an armchair by the fire, and I wondered why she was often on her own. Did she get along with the other directors? With the family? I hadn't seen her argue with anyone, but she might resent what was happening in the meetings.

I walked over to Beverly. "Looks comfy," I said. "May we join you while we warm up?"

"Certainly," she said. "I'm just wool-gathering."

"I'm sure you have a lot on your mind right now," I said. "Between the business meeting and Alistair's death."

"You can say that again. I didn't agree with Dr. M's decision to bring everyone here, but it's his company. I'm just the corporate secretary. And I was his personal assistant for years before I got this promotion, so I'm accustomed to watching the decisions being made, not making them myself."

"It must have been a difficult transition," I said, as I sat back in the wing chair. "I was a technical writer for a long time, and I saw lots of corporate implosions." I thought I'd seed the conversation, so I added, "At one company, the directors moved to have the president declared incompetent so they could get rid of him."

Beverly nodded. "Alistair was trying that himself. He prepared a petition to the Chancery Court in Delaware, where Dr. M's is incorporated, to have his father removed. But he couldn't get any of the other directors to agree to it, not even his sister."

"You all knew about it?" I asked, as Rochester rolled on his back and began waving his legs in the air, the position Lili and I called the dying cockroach.

"We did," Beverly said. "Dr. M knew, too. That's why he wanted us all together for more than just a single meeting. So he could prove that he had the right vision for the company." She smiled. "And he wanted to put Alistair in his place. He didn't agree with some of the changes Alistair wanted to make, and he put his foot down on Monday."

"What would happen if he was removed?" I asked.

"Alistair would take over, of course. Now, I really have no idea. Zoe isn't ready to take over, and probably never will be. So that would mean bringing in an outsider. Dr. M's wouldn't be a family-owned business any longer. But Dr. M is getting older, and he's going to have to make a succession plan eventually. He can't sustain traveling the country and meeting with veterinarians himself anymore."

She shifted position on the sofa. "He had some heart problems a few weeks ago, when he was on the road. It was the third time he's had these problems, so Zoe forced him to go to the ER at this terrible hospital in Brattleboro. He was hospitalized for a few days and we checked him out just as the hospital had a problem with incompetent nurses giving patients the wrong medication. We're lucky he was sharp enough to check what he was being given and protest."

"Brattleboro," I said. All my internal sensors clicked in. "I think I heard something about that."

She nodded. "It was all over the news for a few days. I'm sure you could find it online. It was a wake-up call for Dr. M. That's when he started talking seriously to Alistair about taking over, and that's when they came up against their difference of opinion."

"You don't think there's any connection between that and Alistair's death, do you?" I asked.

She shivered, despite the warmth of the room, and put her hands on her shoulders. "I certainly hope not."

I stood. "I hope things work out." Then I picked up coffee for Lili and me, with a plate of pastries, and Rochester and I headed toward our room. As I walked, my phone pinged with a text from Detective Ecker. "Can you come into the station at ten?"

I didn't answer right away. My priority was my new bride, waiting for my return. When I opened the door, I found Lili sitting up in bed with her laptop.

"I love a man who brings me breakfast in bed," she said.

"And I love finding a woman waiting for me in my bed," I said. "Especially if it's the woman I just married."

I gave Rochester a croissant and he settled on the floor, using one paw to hold down an end while he bit at the other end. I shed most of my layers and climbed back into bed with Lili.

"What do you want to do today?" I asked.

"It's supposed to rain again. I might stay here and play with the photos I've been taking. You?"

"Detective Ecker texted me. He wants me to come to the police station at ten."

"Why?"

"I saw him last night and he's struggling, because most of the murders in Centerbury are cut and dried. I offered to help him talk through things, and gave him Rick's card. Either he wants to do that, or he has more questions for me about finding Alistair's body."

"Even three hundred miles away from home, you can't resist sticking your nose into crime," she said. "Well, I knew that when I agreed to marry you. So feel free to hang out with your new friend."

I texted Ecker and agreed, but asked if I could bring Rochester with me. "Don't want to leave him alone in the hotel," I wrote.

He responded with a dog emoji and a thumbs-up. Then I turned to my laptop to Google the latest information about the Brattleboro case. I remembered that the nurses involved had worked at the cardiac care unit, and if Dr. M had been hospitalized for heart problems he might have been in that unit.

The follow-up article indicated that the problem had been investigated and resolved. A thorough check of hospital records showed that a nurse named Athena Souris had been involved in a dozen of the medication errors, including administering a drug called ajmaline to several patients who died shortly thereafter.

Souris denied that she had tried to kill anyone. She said she believed she was administering digoxin, a medication that treats irregular heartbeats, and must have gotten confused. One of the men who died had been cremated, and the families of the other two had refused to have bodies exhumed for testing.

The Nurse Manager eventually had no choice but to agree Souris had been confused. Her state nursing license was revoked, however, and she was dismissed from the hospital.

The name Athena Souris sounded familiar but I couldn't figure out why. So I pushed it to the back of my brain and called Rick's cell.

"Getting into trouble with the local cops?" he asked when he answered.

"Volunteering to help," I said. "Just like I do with you."

"Did you notice the guy's email address? Is he a real peckerhead?"

"I did mention it to him. Told him to be glad his name isn't Sam Hit."

"Or Brian Jay or Frank Art," Rick said. "Seriously, does he know what he's doing?"

"It's his first murder, and the woman who normally handles this kind of crime is out with a colicky baby. I'm not going to tell him about my hacker tools, though I have mentioned that Rochester is good at finding clues."

"Yeah, he said something about that. He wanted to make sure you weren't a total nut job."

"I hope you reassured him."

"Not a total nut job," he said. "Perhaps a partial one."

"Thanks. That's the last time I ask you to be my best man."

"I certainly hope it is. Listen, I've got to go. I have a series of robberies in town to investigate and I'm trying to figure out what connects them."

"Send me the information and I'll see what I can come up with," I said. "Though without Rochester on the ground in StewCross I don't know how helpful I can be."

"Yeah, I know who the brains of your outfit is. Stay out of trouble up there."

"I'm trying," I said.

Chapter 17
Unpaid Consultant

It had started to drizzle by the time Rochester and I left for the police station. Fortunately it wasn't far, and my down jacket was waterproof, with a hood. Centerbury had a different feel in the miserable weather—no kids playing frisbee, only a scattering of students with their heads down hurrying to class. It might be a dismal place in the winter.

The Centerbury Police Department was housed in an old brick building that probably dated back to the 1900s. Inside, though, it was twenty-first century, with a glass panel in front of a receptionist. The only decoration on the walls was a series of posters about public safety.

I told the officer behind the window that I was there to see Detective Ecker. She tilted her head and looked at me funny. "Oh, Pete," she said. "Sorry, it's hard to remember he's doing detective work now."

That was reassuring.

He came out to meet me a moment later, carrying a tiny dog biscuit, which he held out to Rochester, who grabbed it with his delicate jaws and made quick work of it.

"Come on inside," he said. "I don't have an office of my own, but

Marilyn is letting me use hers." The room had a distinctly feminine air, with photos of a woman and her family along with lots of congratulatory cards on the cushioned board.

"I talked with my chief, and with your friend. They both agreed it would be okay for me to use you as an unpaid consultant. Your friend also mentioned something about your dog."

"Occasionally he points out something that human eyes and noses haven't caught. Like that footprint yesterday. My wife and I looked at the photo on her computer and it looks like a Croc, probably a woman's size."

"I sent the cast I took to the lab in Montpelier for examination but it's good to have an early idea of what to look for. I don't suppose you noticed anyone wearing Crocs at the inn, did you?"

"Zoe Mihaly was wearing a pair of fur-lined ones when I told her about her brother."

Ecker made a note of that. "From what I understand, Mr. Mihaly —as opposed to Dr. Mihaly—wanted to take over control of the company, and his father was resisting."

"I'm not sure that's completely correct," I said. "I spoke to Dr. M last night, and he said he wanted Alistair to take over—but he didn't like some of his son's ideas." I told him about Alistair's desire to increase and offshore production, and widen distribution. "It sounds like Dr. M wanted to maintain quality control and he was less interested in profits."

I hesitated, then jumped in. "Have you spoken with Henry Rozell?" I asked. "In addition to being on the board, he's a pharmacist and he's very concerned about the quality of the products. He might have disagreed with Alistair about taking production overseas."

Ecker nodded. "I was surprised when I spoke to him that he wasn't sorry at all that Mr. Mihaly was dead. He called him a soulless profiteer."

"You could see if he brought any weapons with him from home," I said. "I saw him drive into the hotel parking area in a car with Wisconsin plates. And he was angry then."

He made a note. "I'll do that. What you've said helps me tie together some of the things I heard. And Dr. M doesn't have an alibi for the time of his son's death. He says he got into bed as soon as he got back to his room, though he was waiting up for his son to return the dog to him."

"Is he in a room with French doors?" I asked. "Rochester wanted to go out that way this morning, and I noticed several of the rooms near us have them. Anyone in one of those rooms could have slipped out without being seen."

He sat back in the padded chair. "That's a good point. His room does. And his daughter told me he was fully clothed when she came to his room to tell him about Mr. Mihaly's death."

"Was he upset when you talked to him?" I asked. "Rick always says that it's important to see how suspects react."

"I didn't get to the inn until almost an hour after the body was discovered," Ecker said. "I was busy working with a couple of uniforms to look at the crime scene. We had to pull one of the patrol cars up and shine the headlights on the area, and that took us a while." He frowned. "We don't have enough crime here in Centerbury to justify a dedicated crime scene team, so it's up to us, unless we bring in people from Montpelier."

Once again, I saw that Pete knew what he was doing, he was just learning on the job.

He leaned back in his chair. "It doesn't help that the mayor has crazy ideas about policing. Instead of buying us better equipment, he wants to have us collect samples whenever a dog owner doesn't pick up. He wants the town to require DNA information for any dog registration, and then match the feces to the dog and the owner."

"Would that be a case of poo-dunnit?" I asked.

He laughed. "It's silly, isn't it? But the police operate at the behest of the city fathers. At least this is one initiative my chief is going to leave at the curb."

Then he got serious again. "By the time I arrived at the inn, the family members all knew. But I could tell that Dr. M had been crying. He was very shaky, too. He said he had some heart problems. His daughter was with him when we spoke, and she gave him a pill to take."

He looked down at his notes. "She said it was called Metropolol, and I checked it out. It's a beta blocker that slows the heart rate, so that makes sense."

"Zoe was in the lobby when I got back with Janie and Rochester," I said. "She had her coat on, too. When I told her about her brother she looked surprised, and her first reaction was to take Janie from me and go tell her father."

"That makes sense," he said.

"Does she have an alibi?"

"The sister? She says that she was in her room after dinner, then came out to the lobby to look for her brother. She talked to the corporate secretary, Beverly Johnson, before you spotted her. Why do you ask?"

"Dr. M told me he wanted the business to stay under family control. That puts Zoe next in line to inherit, though her father said she's not ready yet." I didn't want to reveal my internet searching yet, so I said, "I wonder what her relationship was like with her brother."

"They weren't close," Ecker said. "Miss Mihaly said that she has a nervous condition, which is why she has her dog as an emotional support animal."

"Ming Chow," I said.

"That's the one. Her brother seems to have had an abrasive personality. Even his wife said so."

"What about the wife's alibi?" I asked.

"Again, feeble. She says she went to her room after dinner to read, and she was still reading when Dr. M and Zoe came to her door."

"Another pair of French doors?" I asked. Rochester had good insight about those.

He nodded. "There are four like that. The doctor, Mr. and Mrs. Mihaly, Miss Mihaly, and the one you and your wife are in. Apparently the couple who cancelled at the last minute were going to bring a dog, which is why they had the room you got."

"Has anyone told you about Zoe Mihaly's dog?"

"The little white one? What about it?"

"She lost track of him Monday night. I think he probably slipped out the French doors in her room, but she was ranting about how someone in the family, or the company, was deliberately trying to upset her. Maybe one of her brothers."

"You think maybe one of them let the dog out just to mess with her?" Pete asked.

"It's a possibility. And if she thought Alistair did it, she could have been angry with him on Tuesday night."

"I'll ask her. But I've spoken to her extensively, and she seems to be a very nervous young woman. You need a lot of self-control and steadiness to sneak up behind someone and put a bullet in the back of his neck. I've seen a lot of crime scenes as an officer, and her motive would play better if she was arguing with her brother and hit him with something heavy. That's a crime of impulse. This one was more thought out."

I admitted that he was right. "One of Rick's questions is always *cui bono*," I said. "Who benefits from the death?"

Ecker nodded. "Interesting way to look at things." He picked up the scrap of paper Rochester had found. "If Mr. Mihaly was trying to get his father declared incompetent, and take over the business, that gives the doctor a motive. And the sister, as the next heir."

"What about Mrs. Katherine Mihaly? Did you get the sense she and her husband got along?"

"Hard to say. She wasn't as upset as I expected. She was more concerned about how quickly she could get the death certificate so she could change all the property records."

"What about Dr. M and Zoe. Did they have anything to say about Alistair's marriage?"

"I didn't ask, but I will the next time I speak with both of them."

"There's one more person in the mix," I said. "Winston Mihaly.

Grew up here in Centerbury, very athletic, always skiing. Younger son, supposedly more interested in spending money than in earning it. His father said that Winston broke his leg skiing in the winter, and had a change of heart about his future. He wanted to get more involved in the business. He might have seen getting rid of Alistair as a way in. I don't get the feeling they got along too well."

Ecker made a few more notes. "I ski a lot on my time off. I'll ask the guys I know who work the mountains if they remember him, and what kind of temperament he has."

"Sounds like you have a couple of good suspects," I said. "I'll see if I can dig anything up to help you."

"That would be great. Our computer systems need a good update. If everyone in the building tries to log on at the same time they crawl."

I stood and he did, too, and we shook hands. "Thanks, Mr. Levitan."

"Please, call me Steve," I said.

"And I'm Pete. You have my email address and phone number if you come up with anything useful."

"I do." I walked out of the building with a smile on my face, remembering that email address. I called Lili, and she was deep into Photoshop, so Rochester and I hurried to the Cool Beans café, arriving there a few minutes before the drizzle turned into a sleeting rain.

It was warm and comfortable there, and Rochester slumped down to the floor as I ordered my café mocha, then set up the hacker laptop.

Results had come through on Robert Hines, Alistair's co-defendant. He served a year of his sentence, then a few months later boomeranged back to prison on another drug charge. He served three years that time, and returned to his parents' home in Craftsbury Common, a tiny town in Vermont's Northeast Kingdom. His father was a minister for a local church, and Robert did maintenance work there for the next two years. Then he got into a bar fight in Burlington and stabbed a man.

Back to prison he went. And that's where he still was. So that gave him an excellent alibi for the night of Alistair's murder.

Oh, well. I'd learned over the years that no matter what a good a life we lived, there were always people who held grudges against us. I simply had to find the others who had motives to kill Alistair Mihaly.

Chapter 18
Grudges

As the rain beat against the windows of the café, I went back to my notes on Alistair's family. Did one of them have a motive to kill him? Rochester looked up and licked my left hand, where I was still getting accustomed to the gold band on my ring finger.

"Yes, puppy, that's my connection to Mama Lili," I said, and I rubbed the top of his head.

I took the ring off and polished it with a napkin. It gave me pleasure to wear a wedding ring again, after so many years without one. I had to leave my first band in my jewelry box when I went to prison, and by the time I left I was already divorced.

This new band felt better, stronger. Evidence of my determination to make things work this time around. Not everyone was so lucky, I knew. And that reminded me of Katherine Mihaly. Was her marriage as strong?

My program had been able to hack into a messaging app that she used. It felt icky reading private messages she'd been sending to her sister, so I scanned quickly looking for words like "Alistair" and "husband."

I didn't have to look far. I found a long message chain that was a litany of complaints against him. He was bossy and mercurial. He couldn't make decisions, leaving them to scramble for dinner reservations or connections with family and friends. He was angry at his father and he took it out on Katherine. He was cheap and scrutinized every penny she spent.

Then I remembered the social media posts I'd seen mentioning her designer fashions, so I knew I had to be careful with what I believed.

Towards the end of the chain she contemplated divorce. "So glad I didn't sign a prenup," she wrote. "I get what the courts call an equitable distribution of our assets, which would probably be fifty percent of the Manhattan apartment."

So she didn't know that the condo was in her husband's name only? And that it was mortgaged to the hilt?

Her last note was, "As well as half of the stock he owns in Dr. M."

Her sister wrote, "That will drive him crazy. You know he will fight you."

"I know. I'm not sure I have the energy for a fight. But I can't walk away with nothing."

I'd say that gave her motive. A bullet to the back of her husband's neck would solve her problems, though I doubted she'd net much cash if she had to sell the condo.

Did she have a gun, though? I scanned through the messages and found that she'd taken a firearms training course in the city. I didn't want to check to see if she'd registered a weapon, but I copied out the phone number for the New York State National Instant Background Check System (NICS) Interactive Voice Response (IVR) automated phone system and emailed the information to Pete Ecker so he could check.

Another golden came in from the rain, accompanied by a thirty-something woman in a hooded rain jacket. Rochester scrambled to his feet and the other golden came close.

Whenever I looked up goldens online and saw images of the breed standard, it was like seeing a picture of Rochester. His head was square, his muzzle straight. His eyes were medium large with dark, close-fitting rims, and they showed intelligence and warmth. His body was muscular and his coat a rich, golden color. He was a bit taller than the standard and weighed a bit more, but you couldn't see that in pictures.

"They could be littermates," the woman said, appraising Rochester. "They look so much alike. Except Rosie was ten in July, and your boy looks younger."

"He is. Five his last birthday. He was born in August of 2009."

She reached down and petted his back, as he and the female sniffed each other. "I'm Lucille," she said.

"Steve. And this is Rochester."

"Nice to meet you." She tugged on Rosie's leash and they went up to the counter.

The littermate comment reminded me that Alistair Mihaly had a sister. From what I'd seen, he and Zoe weren't close, and she was next in line to take over her father's business. But did she hate him enough to kill him? She wasn't the kind of type A personality who I thought would kill for money. She was more like the second choice for anything.

That could be painful. Always being compared to your highly motivated older brother, or your sports-mad younger one, who was handsome and probably much more popular than she was. Never making much of yourself outside of what your family was able to provide. That could lead to a long-simmering resentment. Maybe Alistair had said something in the meeting on Monday that pushed her over the edge.

I remembered that she hadn't been very upset when I told her that Alistair was dead. She could have easily faked that open-mouthed look, then pushed away immediately so I couldn't see that his death didn't affect her. Pete could check to see if she owned a gun.

Lucille brought her coffee over to the table next to mine so the two goldens could commune. Rochester reached out a paw to Rosie, and she settled to the floor in a big lump, right next to him.

Food of the Dogs

"She's a sweetheart," I said.

"She's my rebound dog," the woman said. "I was working in a vet's office and one of his patients had a litter, and Rosie was the runt. I had been seeing the vet outside of work, and he broke up with me at the same time he told me he was leaving town. I adopted Rosie to mend my broken heart."

"I'm sure she did that," I said. "I had a similar experience with Rochester." Since she'd shared something so intimate with me, I told her how I'd moved back to my hometown after a divorce and a brief prison sentence. "Rochester taught me how to love again, when I didn't think I could."

"Dogs give us unconditional love," Lucille said. She motioned toward my hand. "Still wearing your wedding ring?"

"No, this one's from my second marriage. Couldn't have committed to her if Rochester hadn't taught me, though."

"That's great. I never married. After Anthony I didn't have the heart for it."

Anthony. "Are you talking about Dr. M?" I asked.

"You know him?"

"He's here in Centerbury for a family thing," I said. "Staying at the Otter Creek Inn, where my wife and I are. We're on our honeymoon."

"I'm sure he wouldn't want to see me," Lucille said. "Too many bad memories." She sighed. "I never should have gotten together with him, but his wife had been committed to a mental hospital and he was handsome and lonely, and I thought he cut a very romantic figure." She smiled. "That is, until his wife passed, and he told me that his dog food company mattered more to him than I did. That he was selling the clinic and leaving town."

"That must have been tough," I said. "Was he really that cold about it?"

"Oh, I'm sure he cloaked everything in sweet words. But we hear what we want, you know." She looked at my computer. "I'm keeping you from your work. And I have some emails I have to answer. I'm a freelance dog-walker and my clients reach me through an app." She handed me a business card. "In case Rochester needs an extra walk while you're here."

I thanked her and pocketed the card. The dogs snuggled up, and Rochester kept one golden paw on Rosie's flank.

She picked up her phone, and I went back to my computer. But I couldn't go back to work because I was thinking about Mary. I stroked Rochester's soft, golden head and remembered Mary's anger when she discovered what I had done.

For a long time my ex-wife might have had a motive to kill me, especially after I unveiled her rampant credit card debt. She might have blamed me for the two miscarriages she suffered. Maybe I worked too much or ignored her, and that unhappiness caused her body to resist bringing new life into a failing marriage.

Then she divorced me while I was in prison. I was sure her family and circle of friends turned against me. I was the bad guy who'd flaunted the law with my hacking. They didn't have to know that I'd done it to attempt to preserve our marriage's financial health. It could have all been my fault, and if her life had failed after that she would have had good reason to blame me.

The last time I looked her up, though, she remarried and had a child. So I hoped that I'd been banished to the back of her mind. But what if her second marriage failed, and she blamed that on me, too?

It was a scary thought, and I resisted checking out her current situation. If she was in trouble it was no business of mine, and if she was happy I had to leave her alone.

Chapter 19
Nineteen Murderers

Rochester rested his head on my leg. It was always upsetting to me to realize how much anger and hatred there was in the world. Take any ordinary person and scratch the surface, and you could find hidden resentments and festering anger.

From the table next to me, Lucille put down her phone. "You brought your dog with you on your honeymoon," she said. "That's true love. On your part and your wife's."

"That it is."

She stood, and Rosie grudgingly rose, using her hind legs to push her up. "Sorry your friend is going," I said to Rochester. "But you have others."

That reminded me of Alistair's college friend Robert Hines. He was in prison, but did he have a family member who might have had a long-standing grudge against the man who'd sent Robert down the wrong path?

His father, Luther, was a minister, but after Robert went back to prison the congregation terminated his contract. Luther had become a freelancer, visiting congregations when their regular ministers went on vacation or died. But I couldn't find any records of his work over the past year. Could he blame his problems on Alistair, too? He and his wife owned a house in a small town near Lake Champlain, so he was in the neighborhood. I added him to my list, with the details I had. Pete could talk to him, see how he felt, and if he had an alibi.

I had helped Rick put murderers in prison. Some of them knew what I'd done to send them behind bars. I began to make a list. In the four years I'd had Rochester, I had helped put nineteen people in prison.

Even though the café was warm, a chill ran through me. Beside me, Rochester reached back with his paw to scratch behind his shoulder. I leaned down and took over for him. "Don't want to stretch your legs out too much," I said.

Thinking of legs reminded me of Winston Mihaly, and how he said he'd broken one in the spring, and that caused him to rethink his future, and his involvement with his father's business. I skipped over to the search results my programs had come up with on him.

He had gone to Western Colorado University, where I was surprised to see he had majored in business administration. It had taken him six years to graduate, though, probably because he had spent so much time skiing in the state's backcountry—at least according to his personal blog, which he'd begun as an undergraduate. He was an alpine ski racer, and had medaled in many competitions. He was rarely the top winner, but he consistently finished well, particularly in the giant slalom, which appeared to be his specialty.

He wasn't Olympic class, but he was good enough to have secured a position as a ski instructor in Beaver Creek, Colorado, after he graduated. He had continued to race, up until April.

Wait, April? He told his father he'd broken his leg in the winter. Yet he had competed in races all season, so that was clearly a lie. If he was lying about that, what else? Was he really interested in working for his father's business, or just getting his father's money?

I pulled out my phone and called Pete Ecker. "I was digging into Winston Mihaly and I found something interesting." I told him about the discrepancy.

"Yeah, caught that in conversation with him. I broke my leg a few years ago, and I was chatting with him about all the rehab I had to do, and he got very cagey. I pressed him, and he finally admitted that was a lie he told his father."

"Good job," I said.

"I asked him what else he was lying about. Like did he have a gun, or access to one here in town, maybe through a friend. He said he could never hunt, having seen his father minister to animals, including a dog a hunter shot by accident. He said that he swore he'd never do that, so he didn't know one end of a gun from the other. He was pretty clear about that, so I believed him."

"Did you ask him about his relationship with Alistair?"

"I did. The brother is ten years older, so they didn't have much of a relationship as kids, and he's been in Colorado doing his thing for years. I believe that, too."

Pete said, "I've got to take this call from the tech guys in Montpelier. Let me know what else you come up with."

I hung up. Rochester stood and stretched his front legs out and yawned, his body straight as an arrow. I looked in the direction he was pointing and saw another of the flyers announcing the dedication of the dog park.

Ethan, the guy at the bookstore, had said there was opposition to the dog park in the community. People worried about the noise and the smell. But Alistair had no connection to the park—that was all on his father, who had donated the property and the funding to build the park.

I copied the address into my search box and pulled up a map of Centerbury. The first thing that showed up was a link to a series of articles about the proposed park. The corner lot had housed a feed store until Dr. M. bought it and renovated it into his veterinary office. A photo accompanying the article showed a single-story building with a flat roof and an adjacent fenced yard.

When Dr. M left veterinary medicine to focus on the dog food business, he retained ownership of the building but sold the practice to a young vet who went heavily into debt to buy it. His name was

Jason Evangelos, and he was a graduate of the Michigan State's veterinary school.

According to the article, many pet owners felt Dr. E wasn't experienced enough, and switched to other vets. Then a rottweiler died of a burst appendix during surgery, followed by the deaths of three more dogs under Dr. E's care. By then the practice was in freefall. One day his vet tech found Dr. E in his office, dead of an overdose of veterinary tranquilizers.

The practice closed and the building remained vacant until the year before, when Dr. M had it demolished. He was quoted in the paper as saying that he wanted to put away all the bad memories the property held, and dedicate it to bringing joy to dogs and their owners.

An editorial supported his bid to have the zoning changed to a recreational district, and the town council granted it. A few community members had protested at the meeting but obviously they hadn't been successful because a firm had been hired to design the park, and a contractor to build it.

And now it was ready to be dedicated on Friday.

The weather cleared by noon. I had an appointment that afternoon to meet with Chuck Hammerstein, the director of the college's conference center, to share suggestions for our jobs, so Rochester and I headed back to the inn. The air was fresh and full of negative ions, which I'd learned produced biochemical reactions to relieve stress, alleviate depression, and boost energy.

Lili was sitting at the desk in our room working at her laptop when Rochester and I came in. He immediately went for his water bowl, and Lili said, "I want to show you this photo."

I walked over to her. "That's the bridge you photographed," I said. "But it looks different."

"This is a different perspective, with my camera positioned a few inches off the ground. I took four exposures and merged them together to enhance the light and shadow."

"It looks amazing," I said.

Food of the Dogs

"I'm going to use it as an example in my class when we get back." She saved the file and shut down the laptop. "Now I'd like to go for a stroll around town and grab lunch somewhere."

We set out a short time later, walking up and down hills. We turned a corner after a while and I spotted the dog park up ahead. It looked finished, though there was a padlock on the gate. A signpost announced the opening the next day. "Donated to the dogs of Centerbury by Dr. M's Healthy Dog Foods," I read. "Nice advertising."

The first gate led into a small square area. The idea was you'd keep your dog leashed until the gate behind you closed. Then you could free him, and open the second gate so he could run into the park. The same process worked on the way out.

I was puzzled by a second gate off the entryway, which led to a smaller fenced yard. "Oh, that must be for small dogs," I said.

Rochester nuzzled up to the fence, but I said, "Sorry, puppy. You'll have to wait until tomorrow to go inside."

The park looked like a dog's dream. A gently graded hill to run up and down, a series of paths lined by bushes, even a couple of stone busts of different dog breeds scattered around. Grass for sniffing and rolling in. Posts at regular intervals dispensed waste bags and held shielded cans, like those that had been placed around our neighborhood.

There was even a fountain in the center for dogs to drink from. Puppy heaven.

"I'd like to come here for the opening ceremony tomorrow," Lili said. "I bet I could get a lot of great shots of dogs at play."

"I bet you could," I said.

We strolled back to the inn, and saw Beverly Johnson in the lobby talking on her phone. Rochester tugged me in her direction, as if he wanted me to talk to her. Probably just wanted some love from her, but I let him direct me. "I'm going back to the room," Lili said. "Have fun at your meeting."

"We'll probably end up just sharing complaints," I said.

Beverly ended the call and turned to me and Rochester. "Hello, sweet boy," she said to him, and she reached down to stroke his nose. I took Rochester's direction and decided to do a little sleuthing, so I prepared a story to preface a question to her.

"I was curious about something," I said. "The police detective looking into Alistair's murder interviewed me, and he asked me if I'd noticed any unusual interactions between Alistair and other guests. He said something about a pharmacist?"

"Oh, that's Henry Rozell," Beverly said. "He's a board member and he also consults with the business about the vitamins and nutrients in our food."

"Dr. M told me that Alistair wanted to transfer production overseas," I said. "I know they have lower standards in places like China and Vietnam. I'll bet Henry argued with Alistair about that."

"They had a few knock-down drag-out fights," Beverly said. "Both of them have a temper, and Dr. M had to stop them at least twice on Monday as we discussed the future."

"Do you think Henry was angry enough to continue the argument when Alistair took Janie out for her walk?"

Beverly pursed her lips for a moment, then her eyes opened wide. "You don't think Henry killed him, do you?"

I shrugged. "No idea. I didn't know Alistair, and my only experience of Henry was seeing him angry outside."

"He's a gun nut," she said. She sighed. "So many people in Wisconsin are, at least in my opinion. Henry takes it to extremes, though. He had us all over to his house once, and he was showing off a whole cabinet full of guns."

"Antique ones? My dad used to collect ones from the Civil War."

"I think a few of them were antiques. But he had all different kinds of handguns and rifles. This one was best for deer, he said. And this one for smaller game like squirrels." She shuddered. "I had a hard time reconciling his willingness to kill wildlife with his love for dogs, but I realized that his dogs are his hunting buddies. Kind of like his staff."

"I've run across people who think like that," I said. "A couple of years ago we were in Pennsylvania Dutch country on vacation, and we stumbled on an Amish farm where they bred dogs. To them the dogs were just inventory, not pets."

"I talked to Dr. M about Henry once, and he said that as long as the man loved his dogs and wanted to feed them quality food, that's all that mattered to him." She looked across the room, where several of the board members were waiting to enter the conference room. "I should go. Have a good evening."

"You do the same," I said.

Rochester and I retraced our path from the day before up to the Centerbury campus. The conference center was a single long brick building, and a plaque outside read that it had once been a mill, powered by the water of the creek behind it. From the outside, it appeared that vertical windows had been installed along both long walls, opening up the interior to light.

I walked inside and spotted Chuck Hammerstein behind a desk in the first office on the right. He was in his mid-thirties, with a stocky build that looked like it was all muscle. "Hey, you must be Steve," he said, as he stood to shake my hand.

"Indeed. And this is Rochester."

Chuck went down on his haunches to bring himself to the puppy's level, and Rochester licked his face. Chuck laughed and petted him, then stood up.

"I took a look at the Friar Lake website. You've got a much bigger operation than we have."

"We do. A small campus of about ten buildings, all of them built in the middle of the 19th century. It's a challenge to keep them all operational."

"Tell me about it," he said. "Come on, I'll take you on a quick tour."

He showed me the conference rooms and the kitchen, all of them fairly modern and well-kept, and then we went back to his office to chat. He was the first person I'd ever met who had a job like mine, and the same was true for him, so we had a lot to talk about.

Rochester spent the time snoozing on his side on the floor beside me as we compared notes on budgets, marketing, and scheduling. I had a computer program I used that I recommended to him, and he gave me a stack of flyers that sparked promotional ideas for me.

Eventually we veered into the personal. "How'd you come to work here?" I asked.

"I came to Centerbury for college because I wanted to ski," he said. "Had no idea what I wanted to do for a career, but I had a bunch of work-study jobs on campus and at the ski center, so when I graduated I took a gig working in the college placement office."

He leaned back and put his hands behind his head. "I ran career programs for a couple of years, including a couple up here at the conference center. When the manager retired, I applied for the job, and I've been here ever since. Even held my wedding here."

"I did the same thing," I said. "As a matter of fact, I'm on my honeymoon now."

"Combining work with pleasure?"

I nodded. "My wife is a photographer and she wanted to do some leaf-peeping. She chose this area because she knows Eva Alvarez in the fine arts department. When I saw that you have a facility, I thought I'd reach out."

"I'm glad you did. I don't know about you, but I love this job. It's low-stress except for a couple of weeks a year like new student orientation and graduation. I have lots of time to hang out with my kids. In the summer we swim, and in the fall and spring we hike. Whenever there's enough snow, we hit the slopes ." He leaned back in his chair. "One of my old ski buddies is in town, and I took off yesterday afternoon to hike Mount Morris with Winston."

I was surprised, though I shouldn't have been. Centerbury was a small town and everyone seemed to know everyone else. "Winston Mihaly?"

"You know Win?"

"We're staying at the Otter Creek Inn, and his family is there," I said. "I guess you heard about his brother."

"He told me yesterday, and then I saw it in the paper. I get the feeling they weren't real close, though. Something like eight years between them. I got friendly with Win when I was a freshman and he was still in high school. We both had a taste for slalom, and most of the guys were into either downhill or cross-country. When I was younger I went out to visit him a couple of times in Colorado."

"I haven't had much chance to see him," I said. "The family's been busy with meetings. But he seems like a nice guy."

"Don't let that laid-back demeanor fool you. He's probably one of the most competitive people I know. It kills him that he hasn't won more titles, and that he's starting to lose his edge as he gets older. He's here to suck up to his old man for money to fund one last chance at the majors."

He sat forward. "But enough about Win. Let's talk about budgets. How do you manage yours?"

We talked for another hour and compared notes, and then Rochester woke up and got restless. "I should let you go," Chuck said. "Great talking to you, though. We should keep in touch."

"I agree. There's a lot we can learn from each other."

As I walked out, I considered what I'd learned from Chuck about Winston Mihaly. He was competitive and wanted money from his father. I wouldn't be surprised if Alistair had argued against that. Was that a reason to kill him, though?

Chapter 20
Sisters

When I got back to the room, Lili was ready for dinner. "What are we having?" she asked.

I looked down at the floor, where Rochester had gotten hold of a piece of paper and held it between his two front paws as he nibbled on it. When I pried it away I discovered it was a copy of the menu at Olives and Feta that we'd brought home.

"I think Rochester wants Greek food," I said to Lili.

We'd had such a good meal at Olives and Feta that we decided to drive back there. Rochester was always happy to jump into the car, and Sue Flocky greeted us at the door again.

"How nice of you to come back," she said. "And you brought your beautiful dog, too." She reached down to scratch behind Rochester's ears, but he stepped back behind me.

"You must be a dog lover," I said, to cover for Rochester's behavior.

"I am. I grew up on a farm in Michigan, and we had all kinds of animals, but the dogs were always my favorites."

"What brought you here?" I asked, as she showed us to a table.

"My brother moved here and I came for a visit. I met Aristotle and decided to stay." She leaned against the table beside us. "For a

Food of the Dogs

while my sister was with us, too. We had a difficult childhood in Michigan and we were all ready to leave that behind."

"Does your sister run a restaurant, too?" I asked.

"I'm the only one who didn't get the medical gene," she said. "Jason became a veterinarian, and Athena a nurse." She wrinkled her nose. "Jason was always better with animals than people, and Athena, well, she wanted to be an operating room nurse, because the patients are knocked out by the time they come to you. Lately she's been working in the cardiac care unit, where most of the patients are doped up and hooked to a million monitors, so they're not always asking for things."

She went off to deal with other customers, and we perused the menu. "Your ears perked up when she said veterinarian," Lili said. "Did you think she was part of the Mihaly family?"

I shook my head. "No. I remembered the name of the vet who took over Dr. M's practice. Jason Evangelos."

"The one who committed suicide? That's terrible. Poor Sue, to lose her brother like that."

"I agree." I looked up and saw Sue coming back toward us. "We'd better decide on dinner."

We ordered the stuffed grape leaves as an appetizer, and since we knew the portions were large we decided to share the eggplant baked with chickpeas and tomatoes. After Sue took our order, I said, "You must be happy about the new dog park in Centerbury."

She wrinkled her nose like she smelled something bad. "That's a bad place," she said. "You can't dress it up and forget all the history." She hurried away.

"You shouldn't have asked her that," Lili scolded. "Probably brings up bad memories. Didn't you say her brother died there?"

"He did. But I thought that would be nice, to have a park on the site. Maybe with a memorial plaque in his name."

Sue brought the stuffed grape leaves and said, "I didn't mean to be rude about the dog park. It's just that place has bad memories for Athena and me. My brother worked there, and he had a terrible boss.

The man never taught him anything, just assumed he'd learned what he needed in vet school. And then he just abandoned Jason and swanned off to start that stupid dog food company."

She shook her head. "We both blamed him for Jason's death. I got over it because I was here in Centerbury and I had to, but Athena still holds a grudge. I can't even talk to her about Jason anymore because all she thinks about is how he died."

She put her hand to her eye and brushed away a tear. "Sorry, I'm getting weepy. Enjoy your food."

"I feel so sorry for her," Lili said. "Her and Zoe and Winston. Losing a brother, it's so hard. If anything happened to Fedi I'd feel like I lost a part of me."

The stuffed grape leaves were tangy and made me think of summer on an island. The eggplant was delicious and filling, and we were both glad we'd agreed to share it.

Sue came by to check on everything. "It was delicious," I said. "Perfect after a long day of talking to the police."

"The police?" she asked. "About what?"

"Rochester directed me to Alistair Mihaly's body," I said. "Because I found him, I keep poking my nose into the investigation. I wish I could say I was helping but none of my ideas have panned out."

Lili glared at me. She reached out and touched Sue's arm. "I'm so sorry about your brother. My brother and I are very close, and I know I'd be devastated if anything happened to him."

Sue smiled. "Thank you. It's been hard, I won't lie. If I could just get Athena to move on, I think we could both be happy again."

"What possessed you to talk to that waitress about working with the police?" Lili demanded as we drove back to Centerbury under a full moon.

"It just popped out," I said. "I wonder how Pete Ecker is doing with Alistair's murder. It can't be easy for him, jumping into a case without a lot of experience. I thought Sue could spread the word that

Food of the Dogs

he's getting help, so people will be supportive and give him time to figure things out."

"If he needs your help, he'll ask," Lili said. "Until then, give it a rest."

I was worried that I hadn't been able to find much useful to give to Pete Ecker. Before we went to sleep, I texted him about the fractious relationship between Alistair and Henry Rozell. I hoped he'd follow up on that.

Lili and I were scheduled to drive home on Sunday afternoon, and if I couldn't find anything before then I'd have to leave without knowing what happened. I took Rochester for his last walk of the evening, and let him direct us wherever his nose took him.

The moon was bright and it wasn't too cold, and it was relaxing to spend the time with my dog, just ambling along. We turned a corner and I realized he had led me to the police station. As we approached, Pete Ecker walked out the front door.

"You keep turning up," he said. "I got your text earlier. I've already spoken to Mr. Rozell."

He stared at me. "You sure you didn't know Alistair Mihaly before coming to Centerbury? Have a long-standing grudge against him? You were the one who found his body, and you keep feeding me information. False clues?"

I held up both my hands in surrender. "You got me. Convicted of being an amateur sleuth."

"I used to watch those *Murder She Wrote* shows on TV when I was a kid," Pete said. "They always made sure to introduce the villain early in the episode, and often it was someone who was asking too many questions."

"I'm more Jessica Fletcher than murderer," I said. "You can ask Rick. He often compares us to the Hardy Boys."

"You're hardly boys," he said. "What brings you out this way at this time of night? Your hotel's a few blocks away."

"When we go out late at night, I let Rochester lead," I said, as my dog moved over to Pete and sniffed at his hands. "I was busy thinking so I wasn't paying attention to where we were going."

"Why don't I walk you back up toward the hotel," Pete said. "Just in case that was a random shooting on Tuesday night, you don't want to end up the killer's next victim."

"Certainly don't want that," I said. We began walking back up the hill. "Anyway, I don't know if I can help you anymore. We've already talked about all the people at the company and in the family who had a reason to want Alistair dead. And the pieces of the puzzle still aren't falling together. But we know that someone with a gun and a grudge killed him."

"None of the suspects has an airtight alibi," he said. "I'm just going to keep picking away at them until something comes through."

"Could it be someone outside the family or the business?" I asked him. "Alistair grew up here in Centerbury. Maybe he had a childhood or teenaged rival you haven't found yet."

"Anything is possible," he said. He yawned. "I keep sitting at my computer staring at everything, hoping I'll get a new clue."

That's when the shots rang out.

Chapter 21
Murder, He Wrote

I instinctively fell to the ground, clutching Rochester, while Pete pulled his gun and said, "Who's out there? Centerbury Police. Drop your weapon and identify yourself."

We heard someone running through the undergrowth and Pete took off in pursuit. I stood up, dusted myself off, and said, "That was too close for comfort."

Rochester didn't answer, but he did stay close to my leg. My heart was pounding and I could hear Lili in my ear telling me I was stupid for meddling as we hurried up the hill. We were almost at the Inn when I heard Pete call, "Hey, Steve. Hold up."

"Inside," I said. I wasn't going to stay out if some nut with a gun was out there.

He followed us inside, looking barely winded. Oh, the energy of youth. I flopped down onto a sofa, and Rochester climbed up beside me and rested his head in my lap. "What was that all about?" I asked Pete.

He sat across from me. "I don't know, but I'm sorry I said I'd walk you back up here. That was putting you at risk and that was a dumb move." He shook his head. "Maybe I'm not cut out for high-level police work. I should just go back to walking a beat. At least nobody shoots at me when I'm in uniform breaking up bar fights."

"You think they were shooting at you?"

He cocked his head. "Again, let me ask you. What brought you to Centerbury? You have old connections here?"

I explained about leaf-peeping, and Lili's friendship with Eva Alvarez. "I spoke to Chuck Hammerstein at the conference center, too. Comparing notes about our jobs."

"Why'd you pick him? Did you know before you got here that he and Alistair Mihaly had skied together?"

"I didn't know anyone here," I said. "Lili wanted to come in this direction, and I wanted to have something to do while she was out taking pictures."

"So you shot someone to get yourself involved in the investigation."

I stared at Pete. It was like we had never spoken before, and he was considering me his chief suspect. "I told you, I didn't know anyone here before we arrived. It's just a coincidence that we ended up at the Otter Creek Inn with Dr. M and his crew."

"And a coincidence that you discovered Alistair Mihaly's body?"

"That was the dog," I said heatedly. "I told you. Janie came over to Rochester and then led us back to Alistair."

"Do you own a gun?"

My pulse was racing again. "I do. But it's locked up in my house in Stewart's Crossing. It's a Glock and it hasn't been fired in more than year, since the last time I went to the shooting range with Rick. He has my keys. You can call him and he'll go to my house and tell you the gun is there."

"You could have bought another one on the way here," he said. "You don't need a license or a permit to buy a gun in Pennsylvania."

"How do you know that?"

"I did my research on you. After I spoke to your friend I looked up the crimes in Stewart's Crossing. Without even having to put your name in my search box I came up with a half-dozen murders that were connected to you. Including your next-door neighbor."

I straightened my back. "Do I need an attorney? I'm not in custody here so I know you don't have to read me my Miranda rights."

Pete relaxed a bit. "I don't really think you had anything to do with Mr. Mihaly's murder. And the fact that someone else was out there shooting tonight makes that even more clear to me. But the real question is, who were they aiming at? Me, or you?"

"You're the cop."

"But you've been sticking your nose into this case, asking questions. Maybe someone you talked to thinks you're getting too close to the truth. It's possible that person was trying to sneak up on you and shoot you in the back of the neck while you were out with Rochester. But I ended up with you, so they had to take a couple of pot shots instead."

"Are you going to be able to find the bullets?"

He shrugged. "I doubt it. We don't know where the shooter was, or even which direction they were aiming in. Those bullets could be anywhere. I will go back out tomorrow morning and look around, but I doubt I'll find anything."

"Do you want me and Rochester to help?"

He shook his head. "I think you've done enough already."

He stood up and walked out. "I don't think we want to tell Mama Lili about this," I said to Rochester, as I stroked his head. "At least not now. Maybe when we get back to Stewart's Crossing."

Despite the number of times I'd gotten myself in trouble working with Rick, I couldn't believe someone had really been aiming for me out there. It was Pete they were after.

I kept telling myself that as Rochester and I walked back to the room.

Chapter 22
Dog Park

Fortunately, Lili was already asleep, so I didn't have to explain why Rochester and I had been out so long. I washed up, stripped down and slid into bed beside her, and Rochester flopped on the floor beside me. I had trouble falling asleep, but I must have because I woke to the dog's tongue on my face.

Whatever else happened in my life, Rochester still needed to be walked regularly. Friday morning dawned sunny and clear, but I gave him a relatively short walk, staying to main streets where there were people and cars passing.

When we returned, the three of us ate breakfast in the lobby along with several members of Dr. M's entourage, who were talking about the dedication of the dog park later that morning. "Are you bringing your handsome boy?" Beverly Johnson asked us.

"Planning to," I said. "He's very friendly, as you already know, so he should do well at the dog park."

Pete Ecker came in, accompanied by a gust of cold air. Ophelia greeted him. "Morning, Pete. Help yourself to some coffee and a pastry if you like."

"Thanks, I will," he said. When he had his cup and a Danish, he came over to me. "Can I talk with you for a few minutes?" he asked.

He nodded toward a pair of chairs at the far corner of the lobby where we could talk privately.

"Sure." I'd already finished my chocolate croissant, so I grabbed my coffee cup, refilled it with decaf, and followed him. Rochester came with us, of course.

"Could you find any bullets?" I asked as we sat. "Or any evidence of the shooter?"

He shook his head. "It's like it never happened. But we both heard the shots, right?"

"We did. Three of them. Then you went down and I started chasing."

He sipped his coffee. "Look, I'm sorry I lashed out at you last night. I think I've watched too many TV programs."

"I understand. Homicide is complicated," I said. "There are a lot of puzzle pieces to put together."

"And right now none of them are fitting," he said.

"You were within your rights to question me last night" I said. "My record of helping Rick can look suspicious to an outsider." I hesitated, then added, "You might have been right on one thing, though. I have been poking around, and last night Lili and I had dinner at Olives & Feta."

"And?"

"And somehow it popped out of my mouth that I was helping you with your investigation."

"Why would you say that? To undermine me?"

"Not at all. It seems like all the hotel and restaurant people in town know each other, so I thought that if Sue knew you were getting help, she'd spread the word and people would cut you some slack."

"It doesn't work that way. Instead, she's spreading the word that you know more than you think you do, and maybe someone she spoke to decided to come after you. You've just widened my suspect pool to the whole town."

I didn't know what to say. I felt embarrassed and stupid. I knew how small towns worked, and Pete was right, the news of my involvement could have spread easily to Alistair's killer.

"At least I hope the attack last night proved I didn't do anything more than find the body."

He smiled. "Nothing says there aren't two shooters in town," he said. "But yeah, you're off my suspect list." He sat back. "I got all the forensics results back from Montpelier and I talked them through with Marilyn and the chief. Mr. Mihaly was shot once in the back of the neck with a 9 MM handgun. From the color of the tip and the microstamping on the bullet retrieved from Mr. Mihaly's body we can identify the gun as a Smith & Wesson pistol. If we can find the gun that was used, we can match it to the bullet." He shrugged. "But that's down the road."

"What about the footprint?"

"You and your wife were right, it's from a woman's Croc, size seven. I've sent Miss Mihaly's fur-lined Crocs to the lab in Montpelier to check for a match." He smiled. "She was not happy to give up her shoes. Fortunately I've had a lot of experience calming down women." He held up his hand. "Not in my personal life, you understand."

"I understand," I said. "I was married once before, so I know what it takes."

His face reddened, as if he'd admitted he didn't have much dating experience. But he plowed forward. "I wanted to take the doctor's coat into evidence, too, but he used to treat our K9s and he's a friend of the chief's. So I did some basic tests on it and gave it back to him."

"He's an older guy and needs a warm coat," I said.

"That's what the chief said."

He held out one hand, palm up. "I have motives from a number of suspects. Mr. Mihaly was considering having his father declared incompetent. That gives Dr. M a motive. Zoe Mihaly stands to take over the business with her brother dead. Mrs. Katherine Mihaly admits she was unhappy in her marriage, and I followed up on that gun registration lead you sent."

Food of the Dogs

He closed his palm and took a sip of his coffee. "She owns a Smith & Wesson pistol, but she swears it's in a drawer in her apartment in New York. Miss Mihaly doesn't have a gun registered in her name, and neither does Dr. M. However, as I'm sure you know, there are a lot of unregistered guns out there."

"Nearly four hundred million unregistered firearms in the US," I said. "I had to look that up for something I was working on with Rick a while ago, and the number stuck with me."

Pete switched cups from one hand to the other and opened the other palm. "All three of these suspects have poor alibis. Each of them was alone at the time Mr. Mihaly was shot, and each of them was in a hotel room with outside access through French doors."

"What about Henry Rozell?" I asked.

"He's another one with a grudge against Mr. Mihaly, and even in our brief conversation he got very agitated about Mr. Mihaly's plan to take production of the dog food overseas. And he admitted that he brought a rifle, a shotgun and a handgun with him from Wisconsin."

"All those?"

He shrugged. "He said he was hoping to get some hunting in while he's here. We have 73,000 resident hunters in Vermont, and more bucks are taken per square mile here than in any other New England state. He has a permit, as long as he doesn't use a muzzleloader for hunting."

"What kind of handgun?"

"A Beretta. Though that's not the kind we think was used to kill Mr. Mihaly, he might have another gun with him."

"Does he have an alibi?" I asked

"His wife says they were together all evening in their room. But no one else saw either of them, so it's not air-tight."

He looked at me. "I don't know where to go next. Like I said, I've watched a lot of cop TV shows to complain about how loose they are with procedures. Usually the detective gets some moment of insight, or a new clue pops up, or a suspect admits to the crime. None of that is happening here."

"This isn't TV," I said. "What about Robert Hines, the guy who was arrested with Alistair? Did you speak with his parents?"

He nodded. "Father has one of those nerve conditions, not Parkinson's but one of the others. His wife is busy taking care of him. She couldn't even remember Mr. Mihaly's name."

"I don't suppose Hines had brothers or sisters or a wife who could hold a grudge?"

"Only child. Never married."

Across the room, I noticed that Beverly Johnson must have returned to her room because she was now dressed warmly, in a heavy coat, scarf and gloves. She was with Henry Rozell and another director of the company.

Lili came over to us then. "They're all getting ready to go to the dog park," she said. "If we want to go with them, we'll need our coats. They're waiting for Dr. M and the rest of the family so they can go together."

I turned to Pete. "Are you going?"

He stood. "There's been some dispute over the park in Centerbury so the chief has asked us to show up."

"You never know. Maybe a new clue will show up."

"I hope so," he said. "I'm dreading having to tell the chief I can't figure this out." He straightened his back. "This may be my first case, but I'm determined that it won't be my last one, and I won't let this go unsolved."

Lili and I hurried to our room and bundled up, and the three of us joined the crowd in the lobby. Dr. M was there with Janie and Zoe with Ming Chow. Zoe stood to the other side of the crowd from her father, and I wasn't sure if she was angry with her father or just keeping her yappy little dog away from the bigger golden.

Alistair's widow Katherine was there, talking with Beverly and the board members. Dr. M and Janie led the way and we all trooped out of the inn and down the hill. The sun was out, drying the puddles and wet leaves in the street.

We turned left at the corner in a ragtag parade. We picked up other people and dogs as we walked, and after a few more blocks we came to the dog park Lili and I had seen the day before.

Several benches had been placed under trees so new they were braced with wooden supports, and a platform had been placed in the center of the park. I didn't know what it was for until we all entered the park, navigating the double gates, and Dr. M walked to it.

There were about twenty people in the crowd, along with ten dogs of varying sizes. Zoe and Ming Chow immediately went to the smaller park, followed by a few others with pocket pooches. I spotted Ethan, the bookstore clerk, and his basset hound, and waved to them.

I didn't recognize any of the other people. Neither of the two waitresses we'd spoken with were there, though Winnie and Sue had both been opposed to the park.

Pete Ecker stood in his down coat out at the park's entrance, along with two officers in uniform. It was such a nice day, though there was a chill breeze, and I hoped that the park's inauguration would be peaceful.

I let Rochester loose and he and Janie played together. Dr. M mounted the platform. "Thank you all for coming out to celebrate our canine companions," he said. "As many of you may know this lot was the site of my veterinary practice. After I pivoted to devote my time to Dr. M's Healthy Dog Foods, the vet I worked with let the practice go downhill, and eventually after several unfortunate incidents it was closed."

I looked around. People were paying more attention to their dogs than to him.

"I felt the best way to honor those pets who were lost was to use this space for a park where they can play and socialize."

There was a smattering of applause. "Thank you all for coming out today. I hope you and your dogs enjoy the space."

Then several gunshots rang out in sequence, and Dr. M stumbled from the platform.

Chapter 23
Camel Hair Coat

Immediately I put my arms around Lili's shoulders and we sank to the ground together. I had a terrible feeling of sense memory of the night before. Was someone after me? Or Doctor M?

A chilly wind blew through, bringing the scent of pine and automobile exhaust, and my hands were cold. Rochester came racing over to us, and the three of us huddled together for a few moments. I tried to shield them from any future shots as people around us gasped, screamed, and began to run for the exit.

The double gate caused chaos when all those people and dogs were trying to exit at the same time, even though the two uniforms tried to slow people down and hold the gates open. I was impressed to see Pete Ecker grab hold of the top rail of the wrought iron fence and vault over it.

Once again I was impressed by his physicality. He'd probably been a damn good uniformed officer, if strength and agility was any indicator. He raced across the park to where Dr. M sat on the sparse grass. He clutched his left upper arm with his right hand, and when he pulled back for a moment I was close enough to see blood on his hand. And the visual caused me to catch a slight metallic scent of blood in the air.

Food of the Dogs

Pete had a radio out and was calling for backup and an ambulance. I looked around at the rest of the crowd. Zoe was huddled in the small-dog section with Ming Chow in her arms. Janie was walking in circles around the platform. Beverly Johnson had come back from the street to stand with Dr. M as they waited for the ambulance. Ethan and his basset had made it out and were on their way up the street.

Most of the other dog owners were gone by then and the police officers were more concerned with helping them exit the park than getting their names and addresses as witnesses. Well, it was a small town, so perhaps people knew each other.

Lili and I stood up, and Rochester huddled nervously against my leg as the noise and chaos abated. "Did you hear the direction the shots came from?" I asked Lili.

"I think to the right," she said.

"That's what I think, too," I said. I looked in that direction and saw a two-story building, with a tavern on the ground floor, and what looked like apartments on the second. A flat roof held an air conditioning unit. The shooter could have hidden up there, waiting for the right moment.

As I stroked Rochester's golden fur, I remembered Dr. M's camel hair coat—which Alistair had been wearing the night he was killed. From behind, his light-blonde hair could have passed for his father's, which was turning white.

Had the killer intended to shoot Dr. M on Tuesday night? From this second attack, it was clear to me that someone was after him, not his son. Was Alistair's death a mistaken attempt to kill his father? Was I looking at this case from the wrong angle?'

A siren rose in the air, and quickly the same EMT wagon that had come for Alistair was pulling up in front of the park, along with two other marked squad cars.

Lili had brought a camera with her, on a strap around her neck. "I'm going to take some photos," she said. "Why don't you and Rochester go talk to the detective."

I was reluctant to stand up and put myself in the shooter's sights again, if they were still out there, but I also didn't want to tell Lili about what had happened the night before. So I rose, feeling every bit of my forty-plus years in my legs.

"Stay away from where the doctor is," I said. "The shooter might still be in the area, waiting for another opportunity."

"I've been in war zones," she said. "I can manage to avoid a single shooter."

I shook my head. "Don't think like that. You're even more important to me now that we're married." I didn't want to add that someone might come after her to get to me.

She leaned over and kissed my cheek, her lips cold against my skin. "I feel the same way."

She turned from me and began focusing the camera on the rooftop where we thought the shots had come from. I sighed and tugged on Rochester's leash, and we walked toward Pete. I made sure to stay out of the line of sight from the rooftop to the vet, though.

He was talking with one of the EMTs, who was leading him toward the street. They'd have to take him to the hospital to have that bullet removed.

Pete stood beside the platform, looking around, first up in the air, then at the ground. "Can you and your dog help look for bullets?" he asked me. "It's going to take over an hour to get a CSI team here from Montpelier. I've got the patrol officers heading to that building over there, and canvassing the neighbors."

The sun had come out from behind a cloud and was beating down on us, heating the previously chilly air. I unwound my scarf and tucked it in my pocket. "Did your guys get the names of the people who were here in the park?" I asked.

He shook his head. "Too busy helping them get out. But I recognized a couple of them, and I'll start with them once I finish here. This is a small town and people know each other, especially the ones with dogs."

"That's what it's like in my neighborhood, too," I said. "Though I tend to know the dogs' names more than the people. I did recognize one guy—his name is Ethan, and he works at the bookstore. He was the guy with the basset hound."

He pulled out his notebook and wrote that down. Then he looked up. "I think the only place a shooter could have stayed out of sight was up on the roof over there." He pointed to the building Lili was aiming at.

"My wife and I agree. She's taking some pictures of it," I said.

Rochester was tugging on my arm, and I let him lead the way a few feet from the platform. He stopped at a tiny hole in the ground that looked like it had been made by a bullet, and his whole snout quivered. The trajectory matched.

Pete pulled out an evidence bag and a Swiss army knife, and began digging around the hole. As he did, Rochester sat on his haunches, a satisfied look on his face.

"Hey, pup, your work isn't done yet," I said to him. I gave his leash a short tug. "Can you find anything else?"

He cocked his head and looked at me, and I leaned my nose toward the ground and sniffed. He barked once. "Come on, Rochester. I'm pretty sure I heard three shots. That means there's another bullet to be found."

He went down on his front legs in the play position. "Yes, it's all fun and games to you, puppy, but someone was shot. Be serious. And I'll give you a biscuit later."

The "B" word triggered something in him, and he looked back to the ground. His whole snout quivered, and I hoped he was using all those sensors in his whiskers to find the last bullet. He tugged me about a foot away, then went down on the ground in front of another tiny hole.

"Good boy." I scratched behind his ears and he opened his mouth wide in a doggy grin. By then Pete had excavated the first bullet and he joined us.

"Not a nine-millimeter like the one from the Smith & Wesson

used on Mr. Mihaly," Pete said. "I did a rough measure, and I pulled a 5.56 rifle caliber cartridge out of the ground."

"Different weapon," I said. "That doesn't rule out the same shooter, though, does it? I imagine out here in the country people have multiple weapons."

"They do." He knelt down and began digging around the perimeter of the second hole. "Not to make a pun or anything, but this shoots a hole in my theories about who killed Mr. Mihaly. All three of my prime suspects were here, including Dr. M."

"I agree," I said, as Rochester settled beside me and Pete dug in the hard ground. "I think the camel hair coat is a big indicator."

He looked at me.

"Alistair was wearing his father's coat when he was shot. The coat Dr. M was wearing today. And in the dark, from behind, Alistair's blond hair could be mistaken for Dr. M's white hair."

"I was thinking that myself," Pete said. "Though I hadn't put it into words yet."

A uniformed officer came into the park then with stakes and crime scene tape, and Pete directed her to mark off the areas where the bullets had landed. "There's a specialist with the State Police who can verify the trajectory of the bullets," Pete said as he stood up. He had put an evidence bag around his hand, and he had a cartridge in his grasp. The heat of the bullet had warmed some of the cold dirt into muddy clumps.

He slid the bag off his hand and sealed it. Then he handed the two bags to the officer and instructed her to label them and take them back to the station.

I was chilled by then, as Lili came over to join us. She took a few photos of the holes in the ground for Pete. "I took a few pictures of Dr. M as he was speaking," she said. "I'll forward them to you with the other shots I took."

"I'd appreciate that," he said. "And now I'm going to head back to the station and see if any of these new pieces of information make sense. I'd like you both to come by this afternoon and give formal statements about what you witnessed."

We agreed to meet him at two o'clock. "I'll do some thinking, too," I said. I could already feel my fingers tingling at the notion of going online now that I was sure Dr. M was the intended victim.

Lili linked her arm in mine, and Rochester led the way out of the park.

Chapter 24
Chemistry Professor

When we got back to the inn, I said, "I'd like to call Rick and see what his opinion is of what's going on," I said.

"I noticed that Ophelia put out some muffins," Lili said. "I'll take my laptop out to the lobby and nibble while I prepare these pictures to send to Pete Ecker. You can stay here in the room and talk to Rick."

"You're a sweetheart," I said, and kissed her cheek.

I texted Rick. "Have a couple of minutes to talk about what's going on up here?"

Then I played tug-a-rope with Rochester for a few minutes until the phone rang with his *Hawaii Five-O* ring tone.

"What kind of trouble have you gotten into now?" Rick asked. "You're supposed to be on your honeymoon."

"We're enjoying ourselves," I said. "But we can't stay in bed 24-7."

"Tamsen and I tried that in Vegas, but there's only so much time we could send Justin away," he said. "I told your new detective friend that you could help him. Probably a mistake."

"He'll never take away the title of Frank Hardy from you," I said. "But he's green at the homicide game, and the woman who's supposed to be mentoring him is busy with her new baby. You're the one with the real experience here. I need you to help me direct him."

He sighed. "Tell me what's going on."

I went through Alistair Mihaly's shooting death, and then the attack on Dr. M earlier that day. "That means Dr. M was the real target all along, right?" I asked. "Alistair was wearing his father's coat, and from the rear his hair looked like his father's."

"There's a strong case for that," Rick said. "But you also need to consider that the son's death wasn't a mistake. Who has a motive to kill them both?"

I scribbled hasty notes.

"And you said a different weapon was used, right?" Rick asked. "So you can't ignore the possibility that these two shootings aren't connected at all."

"Isn't that a big stretch?" I asked. "Two members of the same family shot within a couple of days. Aren't the chances of two different assailants remote?"

"They are. But remote doesn't mean impossible."

"Okay," I said. "But if we go with my original idea, then Alistair's death was a mistake, and the three main suspects are all in the clear for Dr. M's shooting."

"Who are those?"

"Dr. M, his daughter Zoe, and Alistair's wife, Katherine."

"Any one of them could have killed Alistair, and then hired someone to shoot the doctor to cover up. You said he was only shot in the arm, right?"

"Yes."

"So he could have hired someone to shoot at him and miss. Or his daughter or daughter-in-law could have. You've got to cover every angle."

I groaned.

"Which means you and your detective pal need to revisit your assumptions. Why would someone want to kill the good doctor?"

"I don't know. He seemed like a nice guy."

Rick snorted. "What did Rochester think?"

"Rochester liked him too. And he has a golden retriever."

"Dog ownership does not equal innocence," Rick said. "You ought to know that by now."

I wanted to defend Rochester's instincts, but so far the only people he hadn't liked were Sue Flocky and Zoe Mihaly. He could have smelled something he didn't like from the kitchen on Sue. And he might have avoided Zoe because of Ming Chow.

Rick continued, "If you really want to help this guy, you need to do the research you usually do. Dig around in the doctor's background. He used to live in this town where you are, right?"

"That's true. He had a veterinary practice here for years. On the site of the dog park."

"So look back at his record. Any people in town he pissed off? Did he kill anyone's dog or cat?"

"I've heard about problems with the vet who took over for him, and I met a woman who had an affair with him before he left town. She wasn't happy about it, but that was ten years ago."

"There's always something," Rick said. "I've got to go, but I can talk to you tonight if you want."

I thanked him and hung up, and I was proud that I hadn't mentioned getting shot at the night before. He would have insisted that I stop doing anything to help Pete, and that I tell Lili immediately. I didn't want to do either of those things.

I went back to the research I'd done on Doctor M. I had focused on his relationship with his son, but Rick was right, there were probably people in his past who had grudges against him.

This time I focused on the time Dr. M had spent as a practicing veterinarian in Centerbury. That was before people began documenting everything online, so it was harder to find complaints against him. I remembered getting the dog-walking card from Lucille, who had the affair with Dr. M while his wife was sick, and I texted her name and number to Pete with a brief explanation.

I sat back. Who could I ask about that time? Ethan, the bookstore clerk, had only come to Centerbury to attend college, and so he wouldn't have been around then. Ophelia and Tyson had only bought the inn a few years ago—they'd been in Brooklyn before that.

Both the waitresses, Winnie and Sue, had mentioned problems with the veterinary practice, but they had spoken about the younger vet, not Dr. M.

That's why it was easier for me to investigate back in Stewart's Crossing. I knew who had been there when I was a kid, my classmates and their parents, the librarians, and the people who owned the stores. There was always someone in my extended network who I could talk to.

Rochester came over to nuzzle me, and I petted him absently. I reached for the bag of treats Ophelia had given me, which Dr. M had given her, and fed him one.

I looked at the label on the bag. Was there something to explore in Dr. M's Healthy Pet Foods? I felt energized, and thanked Rochester effusively. But he was too busy gnawing on his biscuit.

It took some digging, but eventually I found a reference to the company in an article archived by a magazine called *Vermont Trend*, which focused on business news for the Green Mountain State.

It was an interview with Ronald Snook, an adjunct professor of chemistry at Centerbury College. He stated that he'd met Dr. M when he brought his boxer, Mabel, into the practice. Mabel was limping and Snook worried that she was developing arthritis.

Dr. M told him that joint supplements such as glucosamine and chondroitin could help Mabel rebuild cartilage and slow down damage, and they had discussed whether those supplements could be included in her food rather than as separate pills.

Snook then undertook a series of experiments in the college's laboratories, trying to find the best way to incorporate the supplements in kibble. According to Snook, at the time dog food manufacturers were not focused on the problems, so his work was groundbreaking.

I wasn't sure I agreed with that. I'd been seeing ads for dog foods containing vitamins and nutrients for some time, but I had to remind myself that Dr. M had started his business nearly twenty years before, running it at a small scale for ten of those before retiring, so perhaps what Snook was saying was true.

Snook had hoped to publish the results of his experiments in an academic journal, which would enhance his chances of getting tenure at Centerbury College. But he had signed a non-disclosure agreement with Dr. M which prevented him from revealing the work he'd done. He also hadn't done anything to protect his rights to his work.

Soon after Snook provided the results of his research to Dr. M, the vet decided to give up his practice and focus on the business, and he left Vermont for Wisconsin. Without the ability to publish the results of his experiments, Snook was denied tenure at Centerbury and had to find work elsewhere. He claimed that Dr. M had cheated him and ruined his academic career.

That was where the article ended. I did some searching on Snook and discovered that he was now teaching at a community college in rural Mississippi. I copied out his contact information and forwarded it to Pete Ecker. "Here's a guy with a grudge against Doctor M," I wrote. "I know he's not in the area, but he could have hopped a plane."

Chapter 25
Bad Vibes

Lili returned from the lobby. "There's a bad vibe out there," she said. "The company reserved the inn until Sunday, but Beverly Johnson and two of the corporate directors are talking about leaving early. Ophelia overheard them and called your detective friend, who's out there now, telling them they have to stick around until he finishes his investigation."

"Poor guy. I'll bet he's frazzled."

"That's one word for it." She sat on the bed. "What are we going to do? Do you think he'll try to make us stay, too?"

"We're not suspects," I said. "We both witnessed the shooting this morning, but we gave him our statements so he shouldn't have any reason to detain us."

My stomach grumbled. "What do you want to do for lunch?" I asked.

"Ophelia told me about a sandwich shop a few blocks away that allows dogs," she said.

"Sounds good to me. Let's plan to go to the police station after lunch. I'll bring my computer in case there's anything I need to give to Pete." We put our coats on and walked out to the lobby.

Henry Rozell was arguing with Ophelia about leaving early.

"We're not holding you hostage, sir," she said. "Your bill has been paid by the company through Sunday morning. We're not keeping you from leaving."

"Your lousy cop is, though."

Ophelia held open her hands. "I can't do anything about that, sir."

His wife tugged on his sleeve. "Why don't you go out into the mountains with your hunting rifle," she said.

"Keep your voice down, woman," he said to her. "And I can't because I was stupid enough to tell the cops I have it with me, and they've confiscated it until they can match the bullets someone shot Anthony with."

"But you couldn't have shot the poor man," his wife said. "You and I were in the audience at the park."

"I know!" he raged. "But they're treating us like suspects!"

Rochester tugged me toward the front door. He didn't like any displays of anger, so it was best to get him out of there. The sun had warmed the air more since we were out at the dog park, and I didn't bother to tie my scarf or put on my gloves.

We walked down the hill to the sandwich shop and joined a queue of students and local workers waiting by the register. The shop was decorated with original paintings by local artists, and we had plenty of time to look at the mountains and ski slopes represented while we waited to be served.

There was a single clerk on duty and to make it easy on her, Lili and I picked sandwiches from the display and bottles of a local soda, and after we paid, we crowded into a small table for two, with Rochester on the floor.

We were so close to the two women sitting beside us that I heard everything they were saying without even trying. They were both older than Lili and I were, probably in their fifties, and wore matching name badges that identified them as employees at the Anderson County Courthouse, around the corner. The blonde was Eleanor, the woman with dreads was Riquita.

"Did you hear about the shooting at the new dog park this morning?" Eleanor asked.

Riquita nodded as she nibbled her sandwich. "I heard it was that old vet, the one who used to work here."

"Doc Mihaly," Eleanor said. "I used to take my poodle to him, back at the dawn of time when I was still married."

"Was he someone worth shooting?"

Eleanor laughed. "Everyone's worth shooting at some point, darlin'," she said. "But maybe I'm prejudiced because both my exes tempted me on occasion."

She put down her coffee cup. "Seriously, he was a handsome man in his time. And there were rumors he gave extra services to women who brought in their pets. His wife was a sickly sort, something to do with her nerves, so maybe that accounted for the gossip. I only saw her maybe once or twice at church."

"You think it was a woman scorned that shot him?" Riquita asked. "Someone he loved and dumped?"

I thought about Lucille and her golden Rosie. She'd been treated badly by Dr. M. Just then, Rochester whined and nosed at my hand, which held the last of my roast beef sandwich. I was startled, having been so absorbed eavesdropping. I slipped Rochester the meat scrap to calm him. But I kept listening.

"Hell hath no fury and all that," Eleanor said, as she crumpled her napkin and sandwich wrapper.

The two women stood and made their way out of the shop. I wondered about their conversation—could there be a woman scorned in Centerbury besides Lucille? Could seeing Dr. M after all this time have incited her, or another woman, to shoot him?

We left the café and walked to the police station, where we told the receptionist we were there to see Detective Ecker. This time she knew right away who I meant, and asked us to take a seat.

Pete came out a couple of minutes later, and Lili followed him back, while I stayed in the lobby with Rochester. She was there barely ten minutes before she returned. He had another biscuit for

Rochester, who remained with Lili as I went in to give my statement.

It was a quick process. "I got the information you sent me this morning," he said, when I had finished. "But I'm tied up all afternoon interviewing people. I don't see how Marilyn managed all this work."

"You'll get accustomed to it," I said. "Are you going to be able to keep the members of the Mihaly family and the board members in Centerbury?"

"I doubt it. I don't have any reason to detain anyone from the family or the business. And my chief has pointed out that they're all responsible citizens and we know where to find them."

"So you need to wrap this up between now and check out time on Sunday," I said.

He slumped back in his seat. "If I can wrap it up at all. I'd hate to have my first investigation get stuffed into a cold case file. It won't look good for me if I want to keep my job."

"They won't fire you for this, will they?"

He shook his head. "The chief told me that if I do a good job, then he'll find funding to keep me on as a detective when Marilyn comes back from maternity leave. If I screw this up, I'll go back to patrol. And there's no chance I'll be able to transfer to another department if all I have under my belt is one failed investigation."

"Any progress on tracking the gun?" I asked.

"Way too many people in Centerbury, and in Addison County, have rifles. So the only thing we can do is find the suspect and then try to match the cartridge to the rifle."

"Speaking of suspects, do you have any new ones?"

He groaned. "No. Everybody I talk to says Dr. Mihaly was a valued member of the community, and even if they weren't fans of the dog park they certainly wouldn't shoot him over it."

"I know it might be far-fetched," I said. "But I was talking to my friend Rick, and he reminded me that just because Zoe and Katherine Mihaly were in the park when Dr. M was shot, that doesn't remove them from the suspect pool. Either of them could have hired someone to shoot at Dr. M. He could have even hired someone to shoot at him just to remove him from suspicion in his son's death."

"I think you and your friend watch too many TV shows," he said. "I can't even bring up the idea of a hired killed in Centerbury to my chief or I'd get laughed out of the room."

"He was just saying we – and I guess I mean you – have to keep all the ideas in play."

"I'll keep that in mind. Did you dig up anything I can use?"

"Not yet. But I overheard something in the sandwich shop at lunch today." I told Pete what Eleanor and Riquita had discussed.

"I know exactly who you're talking about," he said. "Eleanor is the judge's secretary, and we have to go through her to get anything signed. If there's gossip to be heard, Eleanor knows it. I'll have to stop by her desk and have a chat later. I'll also call that dog-walker lady, Lucille. If Dr. Mihaly was fooling around with her while he was married, there might be other women who don't feel so kindly toward him."

I stood. "And I'll let you know if I find anything."

Chapter 26
Veterinary Mistakes

Lili, Rochester, and I walked out into the chilly air. She adjusted her cashmere scarf, which I knew she'd bought in Scotland on one of her photojournalism jobs. Everything she owned had a story, and I wondered what new stories we were going to create together. Should I find something in Vermont to buy her, to memorialize our honeymoon? Or would Alistair Mihaly's murder be the touchstone we always remembered?

"I have some thinking to do, based on my conversations with the students. You don't mind if I go off on my own, do you? I'll take my camera down to the falls. Photography always helps me focus, no pun intended."

"I don't mind at all," I said. "I'll take the hound with me back to Cool Beans. I have some stuff I want to look up."

Unlike at the sandwich shop, there were only a few hipsters in the café, bent over their laptops with their headphones on. Perhaps that was because lunch hour was over. The single barista on duty was an older woman. I hoped she would be chatty because there wasn't a line waiting for her creations.

"Did you hear about the shooting at the dog park this morning?" I asked.

"Did I ever," she said. Like Eva Alvarez, she had a long gray braid that hung along one side of her neck. Probably a fashion among older women in the Green Mountain State. "That's all people were talking about all morning."

She started making my café mocha. "Have you lived in Centerbury long?" I asked.

"Twenty years," she said. "I started this place ten years ago, after my kids graduated from school and my husband left me. Ordinarily I'd be in the back paying bills but I made the mistake of hiring a bunch of kids who are all in the theater department, and they've got a big production on this weekend. So I'm filling in for the kid playing King Lear this afternoon, and the gal playing Cordelia this evening."

She poured milk into a pitcher and stuck it under the frothing arm.

"Were you here when Dr. M was the veterinarian?"

She shook her head. "No, by the time my two Rottweilers and I got to town, he'd already decamped and left that dope behind."

"Dr. E?"

"Yup. As if we were all too stupid to remember doctors' last names. Dr. M. Dr. E. Give me a break. As if we couldn't pronounce Mihaly or Evangelos."

"I guess that makes them sound more small-town and folksy."

She snorted. "I'd rather have had competent. Can't say anything against Dr. M because I didn't know him. But I could diagnose my dogs better than Dr. E could."

"Really? He wasn't qualified?"

"These days nobody comes out of school knowing their ass from their elbow," she said. "My oldest went to a conservatory to study the flute. Graduated without a single employable skill. Lucky for her she was pretty and she married a lawyer. My boy majored in math, thinking he'd be a teacher, but he was terminally shy. Fortunately he discovered actuarial science. You know he had to take nine tests to get qualified?"

"I've heard that," I said, as she began mixing the coffee and the milk. "But Dr. E had to go to veterinary school. He must have known something about animals."

"All book knowledge," she said. "I suppose he could have learned, over the years. God knows I knew nothing about coffee when I opened this place. But he had a run of bad luck—or bad diagnosis, and he couldn't keep going."

"I heard that," I said. "That he killed himself."

She handed me the coffee in a white ceramic mug that was imprinted with the Cool Beans logo.

"People in the town were all betwixt and between," she said. "Some thought he should have packed it in as soon as he realized he was over his head. Others blamed it on lack of training. But I think the fault was all on Dr. E."

A pair of students came in, and the barista moved back to the register. I took my mug and settled down at a table.

The barista had reminded me that the young vet's name was Evangelos, so I thought I'd start looking into him. It was possible that someone who lost a pet to Dr. E blamed Dr. M for not training him properly.

I put Jason Evangelos into my search bar and the first result was an article from the Centerbury *Daily Crier* from ten years before. It reported that the vet had been found unresponsive in his office. The medical examiner found evidence of a high dose of Butorphanol in his system. It was an opioid agonist-antagonist used to treat moderate to severe pain in animals, and Dr. Evangelos had apparently ingested all the stock he had on hand.

I sat back. How terrible, to feel such despair that your only recourse was suicide. I'd been at a low point when I was arrested for hacking, made worse by Mary's anger at me. She'd called me a loser and a bunch of other names, and I hadn't been able to argue with her.

Rochester rubbed his head against my leg. Had I considered suicide back then? No, I didn't think I had. I was young enough that I still felt bullet-proof, and after I was convicted and sentenced I was trundled off to prison, where I had to focus on getting through each day.

I stroked the soft fur on Rochester's head. I was glad that I'd been able to move beyond that bad time in my life. It was a shame that Jason Evangelos hadn't been able to overcome his problems.

Digging further, I found that several clients had filed complaints against him with the Vermont Board of Veterinary Medicine. The *Daily Crier* had obtained the text of those complaints, which alleged malpractice. Dr. Evangelos had argued against the first two, claiming that he had followed clinical standards.

But as the complaints accumulated, he seemed to have given up. I made a list of each of the people who had placed those complaints, along with the basis for their unhappiness. There were ten in all, but only five had lost pets to what they claimed was malpractice. In the other five cases, four dogs and a cat had been prescribed the wrong medication or been misdiagnosed, but had gone on to live.

Two of the remaining five were cats, owned by a woman named Christine Ackworth. She alleged that Dr. Evangelos had overlooked a deadly tumor in one and had given a second the wrong medication. Her complaint was vicious and she demanded that he lose his license due to his mistakes.

I opened a new window and searched for Christine Ackworth. She wasn't a good suspect, though, because she had died three years before, at the age of 75. No survivors, though she was mourned by the members of her TNR group. Until her death, she had been active trapping, neutering, and releasing stray cats all over Anderson County.

That left me with three dogs who had died under Dr. E's care. One was owned by a student at Centerbury, who had since graduated and moved to California. The other two dogs were family pets, and the families remained in town.

The first name I researched was Genevieve Rosen. She was a professor of English at Centerbury, and her Labrador retriever, Huckleberry, had died of gastric torsion while under Dr. E's care.

The dog's stomach had filled with gas, fluid, or food, causing it to swell. It was a very serious condition, requiring immediate, complex surgery, and Dr. E wasn't up to the task. Huckleberry had died on the operating table.

I felt terrible for Professor Rosen. I could only imagine the heartbreak of rushing a dog to the vet for emergency surgery and then losing him. She had filed a complaint with the state, but that appeared to be it.

The final dog who had lost his life at Dr. E's hands was King Arthur, a pug with breathing problems. It was another surgery gone wrong, this one to remove a tissue wedge from the pug's nostrils. King Arthur had suffered respiratory distress and died, once again on the table.

The dog's owner was Vince Rossi, a Realtor in Centerbury, and he had undertaken a campaign to get Dr. Evangelos' license revoked. He had already testified before the Board of Veterinary Medicine and at the time of Dr. E's death, his complaint was under review, along with those of Genevieve Rosen and Christine Ackworth.

All those had gripes against Dr. Evangelos, not Dr. Mihaly. Only in a social media post by Rossi did he mention that Dr. M ought to also be held liable for leaving Dr. E in charge.

I kept looking for information on Dr. E, and found his obituary. "Evangelos, Jason Mitchell. 1974 – 2008. Dedicated veterinarian and animal lover. Predeceased by father Gus, survived by mother Maria and sisters Athena Souris (Theo) and Susan Flocky (Aristotle.)"

I stared at the screen for a moment or two, letting that sink in. I'd read earlier that Jason's father had died when he was a teenager, and his sisters had both worked to support him through veterinary school. But there was something about the names that rang a bell. Susan Flocky?

That had to be Sue Flocky, the waitress at Olives and Feta. Was that what Rochester was trying to tell me by bringing me the restaurant menu earlier that evening?

Food of the Dogs

There was something else niggling at the back of my mind, though. Athena Souris. Why did that name sound familiar?

I went back to my notes, but I couldn't find anyone named Athena Souris among the people in Centerbury I'd spoken to, or those whom I'd researched. It had to be a name that resonated with me for another reason. I'd grown up with Greek neighbors, and had often attended parties and events at St. George's Greek Orthodox Church in Trenton. I must have run across someone named Athena then.

It was too bad we hadn't gone to Olives and Feta that night for dinner, because I might have been able to talk more to Sue Flocky. Their father's death probably brought the siblings close, so I was sure his death must have hit them hard. And I remembered she had some harsh words to say about Dr. M the first time we ate there.

Out of curiosity, I looked for an obituary on Maria Evangelos, Dr. E's mother. I wasn't surprised to see she had died only a year after he did. Losing a child to suicide had probably hit her very hard.

What had that meant for the two surviving sisters? I hoped that they had found comfort in each other. And Sue had her restaurant with her husband, so she was moving forward. There was one extra piece of information—in her mother's obit, Athena's husband Theo wasn't mentioned. Did that mean they'd divorced during that period? Had her brother's death affected her strongly? Could that have had an effect on Sue as well?

But was that a motive for murder?

Chapter 27
Lost Dog

On our way back to the inn, a skinny chocolate labrador came running toward us from between two houses. He was barking, but his barks were high-pitched and repetitive, with his lips pulled back. That was usually a sign of fear rather than aggression. Even so, I kept Rochester on a short leash.

There were no humans around and I didn't know what to do. Then a woman pulled up in a tiny Fiat with racing stripes. "Is that your dog?" she asked as she got out of the car. "I saw him on Court Street a few minutes ago."

"This one on the leash is mine. I don't know about that one."

"I live around here and I don't recognize it," she said. The dog was skittish and backed away from her, running up to a fenced yard. The gate was slightly ajar, and she stayed as far from him as she could as she pushed it open. The dog ran inside, and she closed the gate behind him.

"I hope that's his house," she said, as the dog's bark changed in intensity, with breaks in between yips. Then he rolled on the grass, waving his legs in the air.

"If it's not whoever lives in the house will be pretty surprised," I said. "But from his behavior, I'd say he's home."

"That's good," she said. "I couldn't see a collar on him." She frowned. "My dogs keep their collars on even when they're in the house, in case they sneak out between my legs while I'm at the door. That way whoever finds them can bring them home."

"I do the same thing. Maybe they don't worry because he's microchipped."

"Maybe, but of course someone would have to be able to read it," she said.

It occurred to me I didn't know who took over once Dr. E killed himself. "Is there a local vet? I'm visiting from out of town."

"Oh, we haven't had a vet in Centerbury for ages, and I'm always worried that a loose dog will get hit by a car and have to go all the way to Salisbury to get treated."

She got back into her car with a brief wave, and drove away as Rochester and I continued our journey back to the inn. I wondered why another vet hadn't taken over the practice when Dr. E died. Bad karma? Fear that the locals wouldn't accept another junior vet?

I was musing on that idea when we passed the Centerbury Hospital. I wondered if Dr. M had already been treated and discharged. I hoped so. If the bullet hadn't damaged any important organs, a doctor might have been able to remove it, treat the wound, and send him on his way.

While I was thinking about Dr. M, Rochester began nosing around underneath a bush. I tugged him away, worried there might be a used needle or something else unhealthy. But he was interested in a piece of paper, what looked like a nursing schedule.

I picked it up and looked at it, and Rochester stared at me and barked. "Is this important?" I asked. "You want to know which nurse treated Dr. M today?"

He just looked at me, so I folded the paper and stuffed it in my pocket. As we walked, I heard the distant rush of the falls on Otter Creek, and I wondered how Lili was doing. What questions had the students sparked in her?

We'd already talked about whether she wanted to go back to

photojournalism, and she'd been insistent that part of her life was over. Did she want to do more classroom teaching, maybe leave her post as department chair?

I tried to recall the conversations that had swirled around us at Guacstar, but Lili had been at the other end of the table so I only heard bits and pieces of stories she and Eva shared, and the laughter of the students.

My mind was still on my bride as we continued back to the inn. We had planned to use our honeymoon to spend time together away from the distractions of work. But we were both independent people, and we'd planned things like her talk to Eva's class and my visit to the Centerbury College conference center to give us time on our own.

Had I let my computer snooping get in the way of our time together? I didn't think so. Lili didn't need me hanging around while she took photos. We'd talked a lot during the week so far, more than we usually did when we were at work all day. So I hoped she wasn't feeling ignored.

I knew that sometimes I paid more attention to Rochester than I did to her. I rationalized it by saying she could comb her own hair, that she didn't need me to accompany her to the bathroom. My parents had provided me with role models of two people who had their own interests, yet came together when they wanted to.

My mother was a reader, lost in her Harlequin romances. She did most of the household errands, buying groceries, taking me for shoes and clothes, dropping in on her aunts and cousins in Trenton.

When my father came home from work, he preferred to eat dinner quietly and then sit in front of the TV set watching mindless shows like sitcoms and variety programs. On the weekends, he loved to tinker in his basement workshop while my mom and I were out.

Both of them worked hard all week, and they often took naps together on the weekend. Or at least I thought that's what they were doing with the door to their bedroom closed. We went to family parties and on Sunday morning trips to the flea market, as they shared their passion for filling our house with stuff.

That was the kind of partnership I envisioned with Lili. But what if something one of the students had said caused her to think differently?

As we neared the Inn, I got a text from her with a photo of the falls and a smiling emoji. Whatever it was she had to think through, I hoped she had come to a good conclusion.

While I was holding the phone and staring at the photo, a call came through from Pete Ecker. "How's it going?" I asked.

"Everything turned upside down this morning," he said. "Now it looks like Dr. M was the intended victim of the shooting on Tuesday, and the chief is on my case. I hope you won't mind but I used your insight about the camel hair coat, and presented it to the chief that I'd already been thinking along those lines."

"Smart move," I said. "I don't mind at all. I'm here to help."

"You think you could stop by the station for some more brainstorming?"

I looked up the hill at the Inn. Lili was still at the falls, so I had the time. "Sure. I can come over right now."

Rochester and I walked to the police station, skirting acorns on the street. Many had already been picked up by industrious squirrels, but more had been squashed by feet and car tires.

I had become a frequent enough visitor to the Centerbury police department that I didn't need an escort back to Pete's temporary office. I found him sitting there with a frown on his face.

"I feel like I'm starting from scratch," he said. "Everything I knew about Alistair Mihaly goes out the window if the assailant really was after his father."

"Not everything," I said, as I sat down across from him. Rochester sprawled on the floor beside me. "You've learned a lot about the family dynamics and about the dog food business. All that still relates."

"You're right. I just got an earful from the chief and I've been feeling down."

"Well, pick yourself up," I said. "You wanted to brainstorm? Let's get started. Who has a motive to want Dr. M dead—who wasn't in the audience at the dog park this morning?"

I could tell he was thinking, because he was ticking something off on his fingers. Then he frowned. "No one. All my suspects were there."

I stuck my hands in the pockets of my coat because I wanted to reach out and shake him. But as I did so, I discovered the nursing schedule from Centerbury Hospital that I'd picked up the day before.

I looked at it, and then at the dog. "Why were you interested in this, puppy?" I asked him, holding it out to him to sniff. "Does it smell good?"

He had no interest and remained slumped on the floor. I looked at the schedule, wondering if one of those nurses had treated Doctor M at some point. I didn't recognize any of the names. But I believed that Rochester did things for a reason, even if I didn't understand that reason at the time.

So while Pete stewed, I closed my eyes and let my mind wander. Nursing schedule. Nurses, hospitals, sick people. I thought of how Dr. M had been hospitalized earlier that month in Brattleboro.

My eyes popped open. He'd been at a hospital in Brattleboro. Was that where the "serial killer" nurse had been?

"Pete," I said slowly. "What if this wasn't the first attempt on Dr. M's life?"

"It wasn't," he said. "Remember? His son was shot on Tuesday."

"No, I mean before that. I don't have it with me, but I read an article about a nurse in Brattleboro who was suspected of being a serial killer."

"Yeah, I heard about that. But it was all just accidental."

"I don't think so. Can you pull up that article on your computer?"

"I can try." He turned to the machine, and typed. "Got it."

"Now open another window and go to the website for Dr. M's Healthy Foods."

"Why am I doing this?"

"Pete. Stay with me, all right?"

"Fine." He typed. "I've got the website."

"Now look at the schedule of when Dr. M was visiting veterinary practices. Was he in Brattleboro at the time the nurse was messing with heart meds?"

He flipped back and forth. "Holy crap," he said. "Was he one of the patients then?"

"You'd have to verify with him. But if he was, then maybe the nurse involved knew him and had a grudge against him."

He leaned forward to read the screen. "Athena Souris," he said.

"Athena Evangelos Souris," I said. "Dr. Jason Evangelos's sister."

He turned to me, his mouth open. "You think…"

"Athena Souris was the nurse they accused of giving the wrong medication to elderly male patients," I said. "What if Dr. M one of the survivors? Suppose she dosed the other men as a way to cover up her intent to kill Dr. M, but she was discovered before she could finish the job?"

"And you think maybe she came to Centerbury to try again?" Pete asked. "But it's a big step from giving someone the wrong medication to shooting a man in the back of the neck. And then getting up on the roof of a building with a rifle to try again."

"I think once a person gets it in their head to kill, they keep trying until they get it right," I said.

"I think it's worth investigating," I said. "Call Dr. M now and verify if he was one of those patients."

He picked up the phone and dialed a number. "Doctor Mihaly? It's Pete Ecker here. I have a question for you." I could only hear his end of the conversation, but he ended by saying, "It's just a theory right now. I'll let you know as I keep investigating."

Then he hung up and turned back to me. "You were right," he said. "The shooting this morning wasn't the second attempt on the doctor's life. It looks like it was the third."

Chapter 28
Eulogy

Pete was energized once more, and I left him in his office, making notes. Rochester and I returned to the Inn, and as we walked into the lobby, Dr. M was sitting at a desk in the lobby with Janie on the floor beside him. Despite the chill in the air, he wore a short-sleeved shirt. A white bandage was wrapped around his left upper arm. He had a pen in his right hand and a piece of paper in front of him.

His shoulders slumped with exhaustion and grief, and his hand shook slightly as he held the pen. "Hey there, boy," he said quietly, as Rochester moved over to lean against his leg.

He looked up at me, and his smile didn't quite reach his eyes. "Hello, Steve. Did you and your boy have a good walk in the fresh air?"

"We did. It's colder than it would be back in Pennsylvania at this time of year, but this will serve as an introduction to winter. How's your arm?"

Rochester slumped on the floor beside Janie, their two golden coats matching.

"It hurts, but I'm glad to have been shot there rather than through an important organ," Dr. M said. "The ER doc pulled the bullet out and dressed the wound, and I've got a raft of antibiotics and pain pills. Right now I've got a more existential pain."

I wanted to ask him what he thought of his conversation with Pete Ecker but it was obvious that his mind was elsewhere. He looked down at the blank page in front of him. "I'm trying to write a eulogy for my son," he said sadly. "It's a terrible thing for a parent to have to bury a child."

Even sadder when you never got to know the child, I thought, remembering Mary's two miscarriages.

It appeared that Dr. M had been sitting there for long enough to have finished the coffee in his cup. I'd worked on enough writing projects in my professional life that I knew that it was hard to get started when something had an emotional impact.

I sat on the chair across from him. "I've taught freshman comp a few times. When students complain about having nothing to say, or not knowing how to get started, I give them some pointers. Would you like me to share them?"

"Please. My brain is so full of what's happened in the last few days, as well as all the memories that have come flooding back."

"I understand. One strategy is to make a list. What are some of the things you remember about Alistair, either as a boy, a young man, or an adult?"

"I like that," he said. He wrote a couple of notes, and I could see the grip on his pen easing as he did. "What else?"

"There's free-writing. You just start writing anything, knowing you can come back and delete or move things around. Easier to do on a computer. Or you could write an outline. Start with Alistair's birth and what you remember. He was your first-born, right?"

"He was. I was so nervous, even though I'd delivered so many puppies and kittens and calves and foals. All I could think of was how many things could go wrong with the delivery." He smiled. "I stayed out in the hallway. That's what they did back then, keep the fathers out of the room. But then the nurse told me I could come in, and Margaret was in the bed holding this perfect little boy."

"That's a sweet memory," I said. "You could start writing that and see where your mind takes you. What incidents from his childhood you remember. Though you might not want to remind Zoe of the amputated leg he frightened her with."

"No, I wouldn't speak of that. But he could be a scamp." He smiled. "Thanks, Steve. I feel a lot better about writing this now."

"When is the funeral?"

"The ME finally released the body and we had a funeral home in New York arrange to transport Alistair down there. Katharine wanted to have the service in Manhattan and the interment at a cemetery in Queens there because she has friends and family in the city, though I would have preferred to keep him here, where he grew up."

"But Centerbury didn't have good memories for him," I said. "At least that's what I heard."

"It was difficult for all three children when Margaret was sick," Dr. M said. "We didn't know as much about mental illness then as we do now. The treatment for what they called nervous disorders involved a lot of medication and bed rest, and that can be tough on small children. And I was working long hours at the practice to support us."

He sighed. "I should have insisted that Alistair go somewhere else for college, the way Zoe did, to get a fresh start. But he had grown up on the Centerbury campus and loved it. I suppose you've heard that he got in some trouble there."

I nodded. I wasn't going to tell him I'd been searching for information about him and his family online, so I said, "It's a small town. People talk."

"That they do. It was a mistake to bring everyone back here. I thought it would be a way to put old memories to rest and start new ones, like with the dog park. But Zoe's much more agitated than usual, and I know Winston would rather be out hiking than sitting in a conference room. Having us all cooped up here at the Inn hasn't helped."

"You do what you can for your family," I said. "And you hope that you get some things right."

"That's true." He picked up his pen. "Well, I should get back to this. We have another big meeting tomorrow to set the agenda for the future, and I want to have this finished by then."

Reluctantly, Rochester rose from where he'd nestled against Janie and he accompanied me back to the room, where we found Lili hunched over her laptop.

I removed Rochester's leash and he went right to the water bowl we'd set for him in the bathroom. I took off my coat and when he returned to me I stroked Rochester's head and a tuft of fur flew off, so I grabbed the Furminator brush and began grooming him.

"Do you ever think about what your obituary will say about you?" I asked Lili as I ran the brush down Rochester's right flank.

"That's a gloomy thought. Especially on our honeymoon."

"I know. But I was just looking at the notices for Alistair Mihaly and Jason Evangelos. And I was wondering what someone would write about me."

"Beloved husband," Lili said. "Graduate of Eastern College and Columbia University. Dedicated administrator."

She looked at me. "Would you want amateur sleuth there?"

I laughed as I pulled huge swaths of golden hair from Rochester's back haunch. For some reason that was the place where the most attention was needed.

"Probably not," I said. "Though maybe Defender of Justice?"

She laughed. "White knight? White hat hacker?"

I shook my head. "I was thinking the other day about people who might want to murder me, and I came up with nineteen."

"Nineteen," she said in astonishment. "Where in the world did you get that number?"

"Nineteen people committed crimes that I helped Rick investigate," I said. "I don't know if all nineteen of them realized I was involved, but a number of them confronted me before they were arrested."

"You do make life interesting," Lili said. "Though I have to say I'd prefer it if we could take a break from murder for a while."

"It's not up to me," I protested. "These things happen around me, and I get drawn in by curiosity or empathy or, I don't know, like you said, I'm a defender of justice or a white knight."

I reached down and stroked Rochester's head. "And sometimes the dog drags me in when I don't want to get involved."

"Yeah, blame it on the dog," she said.

I stood and walked over to Lili, and began a gentle massage on her shoulders.

"That feels wonderful," she said, as she leaned back into my hands. "I forgot how absorbed I can get in computer work, and what that does to my shoulders."

"I know all about that kind of absorption." Rochester rolled over onto his side and went to sleep. "And Rochester has gotten absorbed in all kinds of new smells here in Centerbury. But I think both of us are ready to go home."

"I agree. It's lovely to be able to get away from work and other pressures, but at some point you realize that you have everything you need back at home."

I kept kneading her shoulders, and she sighed with pleasure. Eventually I felt I could ask what I'd been worrying about. "What was it you heard from the students that you had to think over?"

"Oh, you mean why I wanted to go to the falls," she said. She turned over and sat up to face me. "You asked if I ever wanted to go back to photojournalism, and I said no."

I nodded.

"And I don't, not the kind of life I had before. But I realized in talking with them that I wanted to do more than take pictures of landscapes and dogs for the rest of my career."

I took her hand. "I'm with you whatever you decide."

She squeezed mine. "It's nothing so monumental. I love teaching, and I wish I could do more of it. But there isn't room in the college schedule for me to teach photography full-time."

Her department was comprised of working professionals who taught a class or two as adjuncts, as well as two professors who split their time between art history and fine arts. Even the guy who ran the photo lab also taught videography and screen writing.

"So what then?" I asked.

"I might look for the occasional freelance opportunity, something that wouldn't require too much travel. And nothing in a war zone. I spoke to Eva about doing more guest lecturing, in New York and Philadelphia for starters, and she's going to put me in touch with some faculty members at various colleges who can make that happen."

"That's great. I'm glad that you've had the time away from school to think about what matters to you."

"And what about you?" she asked. "Have you learned anything in this time away from Stewart's Crossing and Eastern?"

"Probably just that I'm terminally curious," I said. "But you probably already knew that." I smiled. "But there is one thing that I've learned. Not having Rick around has made me turn to you for brainstorming, and we've done well together. I want to keep that connection between us going when we get home."

"I'm happy to do that." She stretched. "Oh, my back and shoulders feel so much better. I want to try that French place down the street. I'd like a nice hot bowl of French onion soup, and maybe a crepe to go with it."

"*Mais oui, Madame*," I said. "Let me take the *chien* for a brief *promenade* and we can *manger a la Français*."

I took Rochester out for a quick walk, and on the way back asked Ophelia's opinion of the restaurant. "It's my favorite," she said. "I'm sure you'll love it. It's kind of fancy, though. And you won't be able to take Rochester with you."

I must have frowned because she said, "He seems well-behaved. He can stay here at the front desk with me if you like."

Because Ophelia said La Bonne Femme was fancy, Lili and I dressed up. I brushed the golden hairs off my black slacks while Lili pulled on a black turtleneck sweater and a long gray skirt. She added a striking necklace of black and white beads I didn't remember seeing before.

"When did you get that?" I asked.

"Ages ago. In Ghana, when I was there to cover an election. I was walking past a street market and this elderly woman was beading them. It called to me, and I couldn't resist going over to look at it. I wore it for a while and then put it away and I didn't find it again until I was looking through my jewelry to decide what to wear at the wedding."

Rochester started jumping around between us as Lili and I donned our coats. We walked out to the lobby, which was empty except for Ophelia behind her desk. Dr. M had left the room with Janie, though I doubted he'd been able to write his eulogy in the brief time since we last saw him. I understood his sadness but knew it was something he would have to work through on his own.

I handed Rochester's leash to Ophelia. He sat on his haunches and stared balefully at me. Then Ophelia gave him a biscuit, and Lili and I made our escape.

Chapter 29
The Five L's

La Bonne Femme was housed in a long, single-story building that resembled the architecture of a French country house, with stone walls, white shutters over four-paned windows, and a gray tile roof. As we walked in, the rich scent of simmering onions and roast chicken surrounded us, and Lili inhaled happily.

The hostess, a trim, gray-haired woman, bustled over to us. "Good evening," she said, in a light French accent. "I am Pascale. Welcome to my café. Two for dinner?"

"Yes, please," Lili said.

She led us to a wooden booth with high sides. "You are visiting here in Centerbury?" she asked.

"Our honeymoon," I said.

She smiled broadly. "That is marvelous! I came here almost forty years ago, when my husband was hired at the College. He was a professor of French. By the time he passed, I had made my home here and did not want to leave."

Years of teaching helped me listen carefully to what someone said, and I recognized that Pascale, like many speakers of English as a second language, did not use contractions. It was charming.

She handed us the menus and we sat. The menu was classic

French, from the onion soup to the boeuf bourguignon to the savory crepes. "This is lovely," Lili said. "A perfect spot to end our honeymoon week."

I reached over and squeezed her hand. "The start of many wonderful weeks, months, and years together," I said.

Pascale returned with a bottle of water and we placed our orders. I was surprised that the restaurant wasn't busier, and I said so.

"We are between seasons," she said. "In late August and early September, we have the parents who come to bring their children to college. The leaves will be at their peak next week, so we will be busy again then, and after that the snow comes. Where do you stay?"

"At the Otter Creek Inn," Lili said.

She frowned. "You are with Anthony and his group?"

How did everyone in town know that Dr. M and his family and board were staying there?

"We are there at the same time, but only because we got a last-minute room cancellation," Lili said. "Do you know Dr. M?"

"I did, once upon a time. When my husband died, I was left with a black poodle and a broken heart. I went to Anthony for help with the first, and unexpectedly he helped with the second as well."

She crossed her arms over her chest. "Then I discovered he was still married. With children. I understood that his wife was ill, but he should have stood by her. As soon as I learned about her I broke off with him. But other women did not feel the same way."

A bell rang in the background, and she said, "I must return to the kitchen."

"Another person unhappy to see Dr. M return to Centerbury," I said. "I met a woman at Cool Beans the other day who also dated him while his wife was in the hospital."

"He does seem to be an outsized personality." She looked at me. "I see what you're thinking, Steve. Do these women have a motive to kill him?"

I started to protest but gave in. "Well, yes."

"You always think like that. Sometimes it worries me."

Food of the Dogs

"But it's been ten years since Dr. M left town. Would you hold a grudge that long?"

"You mean if Adriano or Philip cheated on me with someone? Would I still be angry a decade later?" She tore off a hunk of baguette and slathered it with butter. "As far as I know, neither of them cheated. I'm still annoyed at things they both did, and the way I was treated on occasion. Could I hold a grudge for ten years? Yes. Would it be enough to make me kill one of them? Absolutely not."

She bit into the bread and chewed for a moment. "But it's hard for me to imagine what someone else thinks or believes, especially when it comes to murder. You've had a lot more experience than I have."

"Rick says there are four motives for murder. The four Ls, he calls them. Love, lust, loathing, and lucre. I'd add a fifth to that list, though it doesn't come with an L. To cover up something or hide something that could be damaging to your present life."

"There's your fifth L," Lili said. "Life. And the protection of it."

Pascale brought our onion soup in brown ceramic crocs, the cheese lightly crusted over and the soup bubbling beneath. We both inhaled the aroma and then dug in. It was delicious, and it was fun to draw out the strings of cheese and nibble on them.

"Do any of those Ls apply to Dr. M?" Lili asked.

"If Alistair was still alive, I'd believe he had a motive to kill his father, to take over the business. He was trying that, with the petition to prove his father incompetent, though he didn't get it filed."

"But Alistair couldn't have shot at his father."

"That's true. Dr. M doesn't appear to have a love interest now, and that wipes out love and lust. Even if one of those women he misled still longs for him, killing him doesn't get them back together. And we don't know of a vengeful husband angry at Dr. M's behavior."

I finished my soup and put the spoon to the side. "I don't think there's lucre involved, because right now Dr. M sustains that business with the force of his personality. If he died, I doubt the business would survive. That means Katherine and Zoe Mihaly would both lose money."

"Which leaves us with life and loathing," Lili said, as our entrées arrived – roast chicken for me and a ham and cheese crepe for Lili.

I cut a slice of chicken and tasted it. "This is delicious." I let the juices sit in my mouth for a moment. "Could killing Dr. M protect a secret?" I asked. "Potentially a life-threatening one?"

"What about the pharmacist on the board?" Lili asked. "Maybe there's a dark secret about the dog food Dr. M was going to reveal which implicated him? He could lose his license and his teaching job."

I smiled. "Now you're sounding like me making up stories for Rick. But there's one big problem."

She frowned. "Oh. The pharmacist was in the crowd at the dog park, not on the roof."

"True, but as Rick pointed out, anyone in the park could have hired a shooter. Not very realistic, I know, but still a point."

We ate for a few moments. "Which leaves us with loathing," I said. "Dr. M seems like such a nice guy that it's hard for me to consider someone who hated him enough to kill him."

I finished the last of my chicken. "I was going to save a bit of this for Rochester, but it's too good," I said. "He'll have to be happy with Dr. M's biscuits from Ophelia."

Pascale returned to take away our empty plates and accept our congratulations on a delicious meal. "We've been lucky on this trip," Lili said. "We've had a whole range of great food, from the Mexican at Guacstar to the Greek at Olives and Feta. And now this."

"You ate at Olives and Feta?" Pascale asked. "Was Sue your server?"

"She was," I said. "You know her?"

"We all know each other," she said. "We have a restaurant association here. We have arguments sometimes, but most of us can reconcile."

"Sue can't?" I asked.

"She has very strong opinions," Pascale said. "And she holds grudges, which I think is unhealthy. Her restaurant got a poor review in the *Daily Crier* when it opened, and she made the poor critic's life hell until he finally quit and moved away."

Then she must have remembered her purpose. "You have room for the dessert?" she asked.

"My husband always has room for dessert," Lili said. "I already know he's going to have the chocolate hazelnut bar."

"And my wife will have a slice of the cherry clafoutis." I looked at her. "Right?"

She laughed. "Soon we'll be ordering the whole meal for each other."

It was lovely to be in that charming room, with a fire blazing in the corner, just me and my wife. This was what a honeymoon was supposed to be—not an impromptu murder investigation.

But we are who we are, and we can't leave our personalities at home when we travel.

When we got back to the inn, we found Rochester and Janie curled up together beside the front desk. He scrambled to his feet to greet me, but he looked like he wanted to stay beside his gal pal. "Dr. M and his family are out to dinner," Ophelia said. "Rochester can stay here with Janie until they get back, if you like."

I knelt down to Rochester's level. "You want to do that, boy?" I asked. "Stay here with Janie?"

In response he slumped back to the floor, and Janie licked the side of his face.

"I guess that's my answer," I said.

Lili and I went back to the room and took advantage of some dog-free time to continue our honeymoon celebrations. We were relaxing when Ophelia buzzed to say that Rochester wanted to come back, and could she let him find his way to the room?

"Sure." I hung up and walked to the door. I opened it and looked down the hallway. My handsome boy was on his way toward me, his leash trailing. I leaned down and welcomed him into my arms, and he rushed forward. I buried my head against his soft fur, and he squirmed away so he could lick my face.

He represented the life we had back home in Stewart's Crossing. I was eager to get back to it, though I was still troubled by Alistair Mihaly's murder and the attempt on Dr. M's life. In the past I had been able to help Rick bring bad people to justice. Could I do the same thing in Centerbury, when I had fewer resources at my disposal, and what seemed like an insurmountable problem in front of me?

Chapter 30
Agree to Disagree

I walked into the room, with Rochester trailing behind me. Lili sat up in bed with her Kindle, so I moved over to the desk and opened my hacker laptop. Once I sat, Rochester flopped on the floor between us.

I thought of Dr. M and his smaller family going out to dinner, probably missing Alistair. I wondered if there was anything more I could learn about him. What kind of man had he been? What life had he lived?

I already knew he was kind to animals, but at the same time both of his children had difficult upbringings, and they probably knew that he had extramarital relationships while their mother was ill. Someone had tried to kill him that morning, and had probably killed Alistair by mistake. So there had to be something about him that caused such deep animus.

Could the answer be in his family? I went back online to search, and the first new result that popped up was Alistair's obituary, posted by the funeral home.

"Mihaly, Alistair. June 14, 1974 – October 14, 2014. A graduate of Centerbury (Vermont) High School and Centerbury College, Alistair was the vice president of Dr. M's Healthy Family Foods. An avid skier, a patron of charities, and a beloved husband, son, and brother. Survived by his father, Dr. Anthony Mihaly, his wife Katherine (Gunderson) Mihaly, sister Zoe Mihaly and brother Winston Mihaly. Services Monday October 20 at 11 AM at Frank E. Campbell Funeral Chapel."

That was impressive, I thought. Campbell's was the premier funeral home in the city, where many celebrities had made their final exit.

I sat back and thought about funeral homes, and that reminded me of the men who had died in Brattleboro at the hands of Athena Souris. I turned to Lili. "Pete and I may have figured out something this afternoon," I said.

She put her Kindle down and looked at me. "What's that?"

"Remember that case that Rick told me about in Brattleboro? The serial-killer nurse?"

"I remember he told us to stay away from there."

"And we did. But the case may have followed us here to Centerbury." I told her about the relationship between Dr. E, Sue Flocky, and Athena Souris.

"Isn't that a big coincidence?" she asked.

"It may be," I admitted. "But it gives Pete a new theory to work with. All of his suspects in Alistair's murder were at the dog park when Dr. M was shot. And it makes sense, right? Athena and Sue blame Dr. M for their brother's suicide."

"But why wait so long? Didn't he die years ago?"

"I think it might have been opportunity, at first," I said. "Athena was working at the hospital in Brattleboro, and Dr. M turned up there as a patient. Suddenly all that old animosity bubbled up, and she had a chance to do something about it."

"Why hurt all those other men?"

I'd thought about that. "If she only killed Dr. M, it's possible someone would have made the connection between her and him. If a bunch of patients were given the wrong medication, she might have been able to slide through without being called out specifically."

Rochester sat up and nuzzled me as Lili thought.

"You think she followed him up here? Shot his son because she thought it was him?"

"I think so. And then when she realized she hadn't gotten the man she intended, she followed up by shooting from the roof."

"I don't know, Steve. It's pretty convoluted."

I shook my head. "I disagree. I think it's very straightforward. She had a grudge against the doctor and she was determined to finish him off."

"We'll have to agree to disagree, then," she said. "And leave it up to Detective Ecker." She patted the bed beside her. "Now, are you going to join me? We are on our honeymoon, remember?"

I remembered.

Chapter 31
Open House

Saturday morning dawned bright and sunny, with a break in the cold weather, and Rochester and I left Lili lounging in bed and went out together for our morning walk. Centerbury was a charming town, and I was glad that we'd visited.

I had checked in with Joey a few times, and he reassured me everything was going smoothly. I'd spent a few minutes going through emails and marking those I needed to handle when I returned. And I had enjoyed the quality time with Lili but I was ready to head for home Sunday. The next phase of our lives together was waiting for us in Stewart's Crossing. If Pete Ecker couldn't nail down Alistair Mihaly's killer, that was on him, not on me.

We went down the hill as we usually did, but Rochester decided he wanted to explore new territory, and he tugged me around a corner and down a street we hadn't walked before. He stopped to sniff a sign announcing an open house that day. The house was a Colonial-style saltbox, with clapboard siding. The gabled roof slanted down steeply as the front was two stories and the rear only one.

"What do you think, boy?" I asked him. "You want us to move here?"

He barked once. "I don't think you want to live in Centerbury. What about all your doggie pals back in Stewart's Crossing? Would you miss Joey and Brody?"

He barked twice this time. I cocked my head and looked at him as he sniffed around the Realtor's sign again. The agent was named Vince Rossi. "Oh," I said. "He's the guy who reported Dr. E for malpractice. You think Mama Lili and I should talk to him?"

He barked again, and started tugging me back toward the inn. "Message received, puppy," I said, as I followed him.

When we got back to the inn, I stopped in the lobby to pick up coffee and pastries for Lili and me. Beverly Johnson was there, sitting by herself. "I guess this hasn't been the experience you were expecting," I said, as I shucked off my coat.

"I've been working for Dr. M for a decade," she said. "I knew it wasn't a good idea to bring the family and the board together, all in one place, for a week. But Dr. M is headstrong and he wanted to do this, and connect it with the dedication of the dog park."

"Any idea who wanted to shoot him?" I asked. I had my own theory, of course, but I was still open to other ideas.

"There's been a lot of gossip among the board members," she said. "Some of them knew him back when he was a practicing vet. As you can imagine, speculation is running rampant."

"People with complaints against his practice?" I began pouring the first cup of coffee, inhaling the aroma of the freshly ground beans.

"Not really." She leaned close. "He was apparently something of a Romeo when his wife was still alive but heavily medicated for her psychological problems. I don't blame him a bit, but there are people who say he didn't pay enough attention to Alistair and Zoe and Winston, and others who say he led women on with no intention of marrying them when he was free."

"Are any of those women still in town?" I asked.

"One of them came up to us the first night we were here, when he and I were out walking around sunset. She told him she was surprised he was brazen enough to show his face after the way he treated her."

"Do you think she could have been the one to shoot him?"

Beverly laughed. "Doubtful, since she was sixty if she was a day, and walked with a cane. I can't see her climbing up to that rooftop."

I put the coffees on a tray, along with a dish of pastries. I tugged on Rochester's leash. "Come on, puppy, let's get Mama Lili her coffee." I turned back to Beverly. "I hope the rest of your visit is uneventful."

"That's a good wish," she said.

Lili and I sat in our room and ate our breakfast. "Anything you'd like to do on our last day in Centerbury?" I asked. "More leaf-peeping? Photography?"

"I'd like to take it easy. No agenda, no pressure. We'll both have enough of that when we get back home. As well as writing thank-you notes for the gifts."

I groaned. "Mary insisted that I had to write the notes to the people from my side of the family," I said. "Half of them were relatives I hardly knew, and she wanted me to write individualized notes. 'You're the writer,' she said. I tried to explain I wrote technical manuals for a living, not charming thank-you notes."

"But you wrote them."

"I did. Dear Aunt Sarah and Uncle Joe. Thank you for the toaster. Mary and I will think of you at breakfast. Love, Steve and Mary."

"Concise," Lili said. "And did you?"

I shook my head. "Mary didn't like that brand of toaster so she returned it and got a juice maker instead."

"I don't think anyone gave us a toaster, so I won't have that problem," Lili said. "Though that photo album with the pink roses we got from Miriam and Amadio might end up in the back of a drawer somewhere."

"I bet you could peel the roses off," I said. "And an album was a good idea for a photographer."

Food of the Dogs

"Not one who keeps all her photos in the cloud," Lili said. "But you're right, it's the thought that counts."

"How about if we go for a stroll around Centerbury," I said. "While Rochester and I were out he stopped me by a sign for an open house this morning run by a Realtor who complained about the vet Dr. M sold his practice to, and about Dr. M himself. Want to play potential homeowners? See if he has anything to say about either of the vets?"

"If you're going to continue to play sleuth while we're still on our honeymoon I'd better go along."

We walked outside with Rochester. The sun was still out, but a chilly wind blew in from the mountains, and as he sniffed and peed I adjusted my scarf. "Are you ever sorry your family came north when they left Cuba?" I asked. "Instead of staying in Latin America where it's always warm?"

"And 'always the hurricanes blowing,'" she sang, from *West Side Story*. "No, I'm not sorry. Weather isn't that important to me, and coming to America exposed Fedi and me to a lot of opportunities we wouldn't have had in Mexico or El Salvador."

She looked over at me. "Are you ever sorry your family landed in the Delaware Valley?"

I shook my head. "I was lucky enough to live in New York City as a young man, and that was a great experience. I liked California well enough, but it never felt like home. When I got out of prison, I could have sold my father's townhouse and moved anywhere, but it felt right to come back to Stewart's Crossing." I smiled at her. "And if I hadn't, I wouldn't have met you."

I squeezed her hand through our gloves, and she smiled at me. We followed the path Rochester and I had taken earlier that day, and found the open house easily. We knocked on the front door, and a portly guy in a carefully tailored suit opened it.

"I'm Vince," he said. "Welcome. Come on in?"

He had the bearing of someone who had served in the military.

"Is it all right if we bring the dog in?" I asked. "His paws are clean and I just brushed him last night."

"Sure. This house is going to need some work anyway. What's a little dog hair between friends." He reached down and scratched Rochester behind his ears, and my dog opened his mouth and stuck his long tongue out.

"Are you familiar with saltboxes?" Vince asked, as we entered the living room. "The name came from their resemblance to old containers, back when salt was a precious ingredient, especially in a cold climate like this where you had to preserve meat through the winter."

"Not specifically, but right now we live in the Philadelphia suburbs, so there's lots of Colonial-style architecture around."

As we surveyed the living room, I concluded that Vince was right, the house needed an update. The carpet was ancient and stained, and the walls could use some spackling and a coat of paint. The kitchen hadn't been changed since the 1950s.

"You're moving to Centerbury?" Vince asked, as we walked.

"We're here on our honeymoon," Lili said, twining her arm in mine. "But the town is so charming that we're thinking of relocating."

"What do you do?"

"We both work from home," I said, to forestall any further questioning. "Lili's a photographer and I'm a technical writer."

"You'll fit right in here," he said. "Centerbury is a nice mix of small town and academic community. Art galleries, poetry readings, lots of people who are interested in culture."

"What about dogs?" I asked. "We've seen some as we're walking around, but I'd have to have a good veterinarian nearby."

Vince frowned. "That's a problem," he said. "The nearest vet is in Salisbury, which is about 10 miles south of here. We used to have a veterinary hospital here in town, but the experienced vet who ran it picked up and moved away, and he left it in the hands of a criminally incompetent one. He killed my pug in a botched operation."

He caught his breath. "Sorry, I still miss the old boy. King Arthur. He was the dog of my heart, you know? I could never replace him."

"That's terrible," I said. "I know I'd feel awful if anything happened to Rochester."

"The guy killed himself eventually," Vince said. "I can't go so far as to equate the death of an animal, however much I loved him, with a human being. But I know there are people in town who hated that vet, and hated the older vet for abandoning us to him."

We finished touring the house and Vince gave us his card in case we had more questions about moving to Centerbury. We walked away, and Lili said, "Just like last night, every time we ask someone about Dr. M we uncover new reasons why people don't like him."

"Though not necessarily why someone would want to kill him. I'm glad that I'm not Pete Ecker, with my career resting on solving this case."

When we got back to the inn, we spotted Dr. M in front of the fire with Janie by his side, and waved hello. I was curious to see if he had connected his own health problems with the death of the other men in Brattleboro, so I hurried back to the room with Lili and grabbed the newspaper article.

Dr. M was staring into space with a piece of paper and a pen with him, and I wondered if he was still working on his son's eulogy. At least there were some words on the page this time.

"Hey, Dr. M," I said, as I sat beside him. "I understand you were in the hospital in Brattleboro recently."

"I was. Problem with my ticker."

Rochester nosed Janie, and she rolled on her back. While he sniffed her, I handed Dr. M the newspaper article. "Were you hospitalized in Brattleboro around this time?"

He scanned through it as Janie rolled onto her side and Rochester slumped down beside her. "I didn't realize it had made the news," he said, as he looked back at me. "I spoke to the police and they said they didn't have enough evidence to prosecute. That the hospital was willing to call what happened to me a medication error."

"I think it was more than that," I said. "Look at the name of the nurse involved."

He did. "Athena. I remember her. Dark-haired beauty. Very interested in my condition. We talked quite a bit about it."

"What if I told you her maiden name was Evangelos. Would that mean something to you?"

He cocked his head. "Evangelos? Any relation to Jason?"

"His sister," I said.

He sat back in his chair, his hand dangling down toward Janie. The golden looked up and licked his fingers.

"I never met her when Jason was alive," he said. "By the time Jason died I had long since left Centerbury, and though he had been my colleague I didn't see the need to go to his funeral, even though I was notified of it. It was in a small town in Michigan, and I didn't know any of his family. I might have sent them a note of condolence, but I don't recall."

"I have this idea," I said. "Maybe it's crazy. But I think it's possible that this nurse, Athena, had a grudge against you because of the death of her brother."

"A lot of people did blame me," he said. "They said I had made a mistake by leaving him in charge when he didn't have enough hands-on work. I admit, he was green. They teach you the science in veterinary school, but not the practice. You might understand how a particular organ works in principle, but it takes experience to recognize what's wrong with it when you're confronted with a sick animal."

"Is that why he made so many mistakes?"

He nodded. "I think so. And if I'd still been around, I might have caught most of them, or dealt with the animal myself. But I think it's a stretch to hold me responsible for his suicide."

"What if Athena disagreed?" I asked. "And when she saw you in the hospital, she took an opportunity to exact revenge?"

"What about those other men?"

"Could they have been a way to camouflage her interest in you?" I asked. "You could have been one of the men who died, and she would have walked away with a slap on the wrist."

"This is very upsetting," he said. Rochester scrambled to his feet and leaned against Dr. M's leg, and the doctor stroked the back of his head.

"I'm afraid I have an idea that might be more upsetting," I said. "What if she's the one who came after you yesterday?"

Chapter 32
The Nurse

Dr. M's face paled. "But she's a nurse," he said. His hand on Rochester's back stilled. "They're supposed to care for patients."

"She's also a human being," I said. "With emotions. Perhaps seeing you in the hospital brought back memories of her brother's death."

"She did seem very interested in my work as a veterinarian," he said. "She asked me a lot of questions about why I left to work on the dog food and what happened to my practice afterward."

"I think you ought to talk to Detective Ecker," I said. "I mentioned this to him last night and he said he'd do some research. I'm sure he's going to call you."

"It's Saturday."

"Yes, and you're leaving tomorrow," I said. "You could still be in danger."

"You think so?"

I realized I had to spell it out for him. "What Athena did in Brattleboro might be considered an accident. But then Alistair left the hotel on Tuesday night wearing your coat. It's possible that the police have been wrong all along, and he wasn't the killer's intended victim. You were."

His face paled. "You mean someone killed my son because they thought he was me?"

"I'm afraid so."

His shoulders shrank, and for the first time I saw him as an elderly man. The lines on his face seemed to deepen, and his body language collapsed. I reached over and put my arm around his shoulders. "It's not your fault, though," I said. "You had no way of knowing what was going to happen."

"I should have had my eyes open," he said. "Starting in Brattleboro. I let the circumstances mislead me, thinking it was all an accident. I was just grateful that I was able to escape the hospital with my health intact. I never considered that the nurse administered the wrong medicine to me on purpose."

"Again, you didn't know who Athena was or what her connection to you was. The police there had a different idea, and they convinced you of it."

I took a deep breath. "Athena has a sister here in Centerbury, too. Sue Flocky, who runs the Greek restaurant. It's possible Athena is here in town, maybe staying with her sister. I'm sure Pete is going to talk to Sue and see what she thinks, and if she's heard from her sister."

His shoulders shook. "I don't know what to do."

"Stay here in the hotel," I said. "Maybe get Zoe or Winston to sit with you while you wait for Detective Ecker to call."

He nodded. "I can do that." He picked up his phone. "I'll call Winston. Zoe's too frail right now, but Winston is stronger."

"I don't know," I said. "I've seen Zoe with you since she got Ming Chow back, and I think she's getting stronger. It's possible that with Alistair as a buffer for her against the world, she could avoid facing things. But I'll bet she's going to get even stronger in the future, especially if you have her and Winston work together for your business."

"You know, you're right," he said. "With Alistair gone, Zoe has stepped up in meetings. She has voiced her opinions in a way that she wouldn't when Alistair was there to shut her down. I admit, I let him do that on a few occasions. It will be a shame if it takes her brother's death to help her face the world, but that's the way people are sometimes."

I stood as he hit a speed dial button on his phone, and tugged on Rochester's leash. He didn't want to leave the lobby. Maybe because he knew Dr. M needed support, or because he was enjoying spending the time with his gal pal. But I wanted to give Dr. M privacy to speak with his son and explain what I'd told him. I hoped that Winston would be upset enough about his brother, and sympathetic enough, to help his father through what was going to be a difficult time.

I went back to the room where Lili had started packing up so that we'd be ready to leave early on Sunday morning. I sat at the desk, opened my laptop, and went to the website for Dr. M's Healthy Dog Foods, where I'd suggested Pete review the doctor's travel itinerary.

He had been in Brattleboro three weeks before, speaking to a meeting of veterinarians from the southern part of the state. He had another meeting set up three days later, in Worcester, Massachusetts, which had been cancelled, as had one in Springfield three days after that.

So Dr. M was in the hospital in Brattleboro after the meeting with Vermont vets, and had to cancel the next two appointments. He'd been well enough to attend a meeting in Concord, New Hampshire, a couple of days after that. It appeared that he'd then come to Centerbury for his meeting.

That fit with the date Athena had been arrested, during the days after Dr. M had met with the vets, probably while he was still in the hospital. I shut down the laptop and helped Lili with the packing.

As we were working, Pete Ecker called. "I spoke to Doctor M and he confirmed that Athena Souris was his nurse in Brattleboro. According to the hospital, she's on a leave of absence, but she's not answering her cell phone."

"She has a sister here in town," I said. "Sue Flocky of Olives and

Feta. She might know how to get hold of Athena. And she might even know if Athena has been in town."

"That's a good idea. I'll head over to restaurant and see what Sue has to say."

By then we'd finished what we could pack, and Lili was engrossed in some photo manipulation, so I took Rochester out for a long walk. It was our last chance to see more of the town, so we made a couple of different turns, passing college dorms, a strip shopping center, and an Irish pub. Then, because I was curious, we passed by Olives and Feta.

The sun was out and I was warm in my parka, so I undid my scarf and stuffed it in my pocket. As I did, Pete stepped out of the front door of the restaurant, beneath the blue-and-white Greek flag.

He spotted us as Rochester was peeing. "You keep turning up," he said.

"Did you speak to Sue?" I asked.

He nodded. "I did. I can't say she was very forthcoming, though."

"What did she say about her sister?"

"Just that she had some trouble at work and was taking time off."

"She didn't say she knew what the trouble was?"

He shook his head. "No, she said Athena has always been hot-tempered, and she'd learned the best way to deal with her was too avoid asking too many questions. She said that Athena said something about the Caribbean but didn't know what island or have a way to get in touch with her."

"Sounds suspicious to me," I said. "Can you check with passport control or something to see if she crossed a border? Or call the cops in Brattleboro and see if they're keeping tabs on her?"

"It's a Saturday afternoon," he said. "I doubt I could reach anyone with any authority. But I'll talk to the chief on Monday morning and see what he says. I counseled Dr. Mihaly to keep close to the inn and minimize any further threats."

"I told him the same thing," I said. "I suggested he get his son or his daughter to stay with him. But what are you doing about her as a suspect in Alistair Mihaly's murder?"

"That's still an open case, and it will stay open until the chief tells me to close it."

I didn't like that answer, but it sounded a lot like something Rick would say, so I let it go. "Well, I've got to get Rochester back to the inn. If I don't see you again before we leave, it's been nice getting to know you."

I stuck out my hand, and he shook it. "Same here," he said. "Your friend back home is lucky to have you as a resource. And talking with you has been very helpful to me. I feel like I'm growing into this job. Even if I can't nail down who killed Mr. Mihaly, I feel more confident about my abilities. I already signed up for an online course in computer forensics so I don't have to depend on other people to do my searching for me."

"That's a great idea," I said. "And you have my contact information. Feel free to give me a call sometime if you want to brainstorm."

"I'll do that," he said, and smiled. Then he turned away, toward the police station.

Rochester and I walked back to the inn, where we found Lili sitting up in bed reading. "Discover any new clues while you were out?" she asked.

I shucked my parka. "Nope. Not that I expected to. I think Pete Ecker needs to be pushing harder to find Athena Souris, but it's not up to me."

"You really think she did it?"

I sat on the bed next to her. "All the clues point there. She made a previous attempt on Dr. M's life at the hospital in Brattleboro. When that didn't work out I think she followed him up here to try again."

"How would she know where he was going?"

"Her sister Sue knew Dr. M and his family and the corporate board are staying here at the inn. Easy enough for her to tell Athena."

"Could she be an accomplice?" Lili asked.

"Quite possibly. Jason Evangelos was her brother, too. And if

Athena got it in her head to extract revenge for Jason's death, she could have found out Dr. M was here and decided to drive up. The dog park is where the veterinary hospital used to be, so Athena knew about it, or could have heard about it from Sue."

"I'd feel terrible if something happened to Fedi," Lili said. "He's my little brother, so I looked out for him when we were kids. But we both grew up and went our separate ways. I love him, but I don't know that I'd risk my life or my freedom to exact revenge on someone who hurt him."

"If there's one thing I've learned from working with Rick, it's that you never know how far someone will go when they're pushed."

Rochester jumped up on the bed then and nestled his way between us, and I petted him and thought while Lili read.

What would I do if someone hurt her, or Rochester? It wasn't something I wanted to consider, because I knew how I'd gotten in trouble trying to look after Mary.

Chapter 33
Everybody Hurts

As we were relaxing, Rick called. I was tempted to tell him everything that had happened since our last call, including the way that Pete had accused me, but that could wait until I was back home and sitting across from Rick at the Drunken Hessian with a couple of beers in front of us.

"Everything OK?" I asked.

"Vandalism at Crossing Manor last night," he said. That was the rehab and nursing facility on edge of Stewart's Crossing. I'd been there a couple of times when my parents' friend, Edith Passis, who also had been my piano teacher, was there for a while.

"What happened?"

"They keep a lot of drugs on site, though they're in a locked cabinet," he said. "There are only two staffers on the night shift, and around one o'clock they were both assisting patients who needed to use the rest rooms."

I sat back in the bed, with Rochester's head heavy on my lap.

"Someone jimmied the rear door lock and got into the pharmacy room. Cut the padlock off the drugs cabinet and made off with a lot of oxycodone and fentanyl."

"Wow."

Food of the Dogs

"The chief is on vacation, and you know Jerry is useless when it comes to brainstorming, so I thought I'd call you."

That was a nice compliment, though it was true the other detective, Jerry Vickers, didn't have much imagination. He was a good, plodding cop but ask him for ideas on why someone would commit a crime, and he'd come up blank.

"My first thought would be an inside job," I said. "There was no alarm on the back door? If I recall correctly there was at least one wing where you had to have a code to go in or out."

"Yeah, that's the memory care unit," he said. "This door isn't for patient or visitor use and the lock is a standard combination. Apparently to make it easy to for the staff to remember, the code is 19069."

"The Stewart's Crossing zip code. Which anyone could figure out."

"Exactly. Taking care of old people is a low-paid, high stress job, so there's a lot of turnover. The administrator gave me over a dozen names of ex-employees who could have gotten in."

"Not to mention their friends and family or greater circle. All it takes is one former employee to mention how dumb it is to use the zip code at the door, and the word could spread through circles of addicts who need their next fix."

"Yeah, that's what I'm thinking, too," Rick said.

"How about the lock on the cabinet? How was that opened?"

"Standard padlock. Someone took a hacksaw to the shackle. Metal shavings on the floor, though they walked off with the broken lock, probably because of fingerprints."

"It takes some strength to use a hacksaw like that," I said. "You think it had to be a man?"

"I don't know. One of the requirements for the CNAs is you have to be able to lift a hundred-fifty-pound person, though they have straps to use for leverage. So most of the people on my list are probably pretty strong."

"Whoever broke in had to know the way the place works," I said.

"That both aides would be assisting patients. Are they busy all night?"

"No, I asked that. Usually at least one of them stays at the nurse's station. Only once or twice a night are they both with patients."

"Can you get a subpoena for the cell phones of the two people on duty?"

"I'd need a reason."

I scratched behind Rochester's ears. "Say one of the aides has an accomplice outside. She waits until she and the other aide are with patients, and she calls the person waiting by the door."

"That's an interesting idea," he said. "And nurses and aides have access to the medication cabinet, so they'd know when the supplies come in. I'll put together that subpoena. Thanks."

"My pleasure. By the way, I did end up involved in that case you told me about in Brattleboro before we left town." I explained my theory that Athena Souris was behind the attacks on Dr. M and his son.

"You have a nose for trouble, Joe Hardy," Rick said.

"The connection between your case and this one reminds me that any time you end up in the health care system, you're vulnerable. Dr. M was attacked by a nurse. The people who work at Crossing Manor turn over frequently, and the facility could be victimized."

Athena Souris had exploited her position of trust as a nurse to get close to her victims. Was the Crossing Manor thief similarly hiding behind a facade of caregiving?

"It seems like there's a pattern emerging," I said slowly. "Though Stewart's Crossing and Centerbury are miles apart, criminals are infiltrating medical institutions, abusing their power and access. It's a disturbing trend."

Rick sighed. "You're not wrong. But remember, this attack on Dr. M is not your problem."

"True. Keep me posted on Crossing Manor, though. If there's anything I can do to help, I'm willing."

"Will do. And hey, be careful up there. Sounds like Athena is playing for keeps."

I assured him I would, but as I hung up, a chill ran down my spine. Athena had already proven her willingness to strike at the heart of institutions meant to protect and heal. She could have been the person who shot at me and Pete. If she was still at large, who knew what her next move might be? I hoped that Pete Ecker could find her before she tried something else.

Lili and I decided to head to a burger place that had good reviews for our last dinner in Centerbury, and we left Rochester with Tyson, who was manning the front desk while Ophelia worked in the kitchen to create a final meal for Dr. Mihaly and his crew. Of course he had treats for Rochester, and my big golden took to him right away.

"Traitor," I muttered under my breath as Lili and I walked out.

The burger place had a lively bar with a bluegrass band, and when they took a break Lili and I had a chance to talk as we ate our burgers and shared a plate of waffle fries. "Are you happy we came to Centerbury for our honeymoon?" I asked.

"I got to take some great photos," Lili said. "I really love the shot of Rochester in front of his namesake town sign."

"He does deserve to have a town named after him," I said. "Though it probably was named after a human."

"We could have let our academic responsibilities keep us from taking the time away, so I'm glad we put them aside to take this week off. Centerbury is a nice town, despite the crime wave that seems to follow you everywhere. I love the Inn, and everyone in town has been very nice."

"Except for that one person with a rifle," I said. "Who could actually be someone who was nice to us."

"There's always that front we put up between us and others." Lili smiled. "Over the years, we've been taking down those walls between us, as we get to know each other better and share more experiences. The honeymoon has been good for that, too."

"I think so, too."

"And being so close to you all the time has shown me more of what you do when you're investigating something. It's interesting, and I hope I've been able to help you."

"You have. Your photography skills came in very handy when Rochester found that footprint, and your photos were able to help Pete Ecker establish the trajectory of the bullets. It has been interesting to brainstorm with you, too, because you're smart and inquisitive and sometimes see things differently than from me."

I lifted my glass in a toast. "I sincerely hope that I won't get involved in more murders, but if I do, it's good to know that I can count on you to be supportive and to help when you can."

"That's what marriage is all about, isn't it?" She reached over and squeezed my hand. Then she snagged the last waffle fry.

The band came back from their break. The lead vocalist took the microphone. "In honor of all the nurses in the audience, here's "Everybody Hurts" by REM." I loved the message of the song, encouraging us to hold on when we were hurting.

"Want to dance?" I asked Lili.

"Twice in one week," she said, laughing. We had not danced much in our past, but we'd both enjoyed it at the wedding. "Why not."

A group of young women, and a few men, crowded the dance floor, throwing themselves around with abandon. Medicine, whether human or veterinary, was a tough job, and the people practicing it faced pain and death every day, so I was glad they had the outlet to throw those cares away for a few minutes.

While we were on the dance floor with them, we felt part of their community. And what Lili and I did as educators was not too different—we were all there to help people. It was important to have a community around you whether you were taking care of patients, teaching students, or solving crimes.

By the time the song ended, we'd stretched those forty-year-old muscles and enjoyed the sense of euphoria that dancing could bring.

Food of the Dogs

But I was ready to sit the next song out and share a hot fudge sundae with my wife.

On the way out, I bought a small bag of pork rinds for Rochester. I wouldn't give him the whole bag at once because I didn't want to cause any digestive problems, but I knew I could safely parcel a few out on the long drive home. And he deserved a reward for all he had done to help Pete Ecker with his case.

Lili and I walked back to the inn, and I was sure, based on all the signs the universe was sending me, that Pete Ecker was going to collar Athena Souris at some point and charge her with the attacks in Centerbury.

Chapter 34
Behind the Hedge

Sunday morning, Rochester and I went out for one last walk around Centerbury. The cold weather had caused many of the trees to turn color and some to begin dropping their leaves. The oaks had gone red, while the hickories were a golden bronze. The maples ranged from brilliant scarlet to a glowing yellow.

It was a beautiful pageant, and I was glad that we'd be heading south, so we'd be able to see those colors for a few more weeks. The silhouette of a mountain rose in the distance, and I saw the manicured lane of a ski run under the towers of a lift. I liked the mountains, and growing up in the Delaware Valley had given me an appreciation for the ups and downs of local hills. But I was more drawn to the littoral, the river shore and the ocean in the not-too-far distance.

Home is more than where you hang your hat. For many of us, it's the landscape where we were raised, the spring lilacs, summer berries, and autumn pumpkins reminding us of the seasons. Centerbury had its own beauty, but my heart was in Stewart's Crossing.

A steady stream of mostly older people in dress clothes were headed into the white church with the tall steeple. It was sweet to see little girls in fancy dresses and boys in polished shoes, all of them bundled under parkas. Winter was coming, to us a few weeks later than it came to Vermont, but it was coming all the same.

Lili and I would have the warmth of El Salvador, and of her family's embrace, to look forward to. The older I got, the more the lure of warm climes wrestled with my love of Bucks County. But with Lili by my side, we'd figure the future out as it arrived.

Rochester and I did one last circle around the inn, watching the water of Otter Creek burble past. A skein of blackbirds flew past us, heading south, as we would be soon. The hills around Centerbury were preparing for their winter hibernation. I was sure that there were deer and bears and other wildlife up there, and I was glad we'd been able to confine ourselves to human predators rather than other animals.

It had been a very eventful week, between discovering Alistair's body, retrieving Ming Chow from the water, getting shot at, and then witnessing the attack on Dr. M. I had been reminded of the difficult and dangerous people I had faced in my life, from my ex-wife to the guys in my prison cell block to the murderers lurking among us in Stewart's Crossing. Lili was right; I couldn't get away from all that. It was part of me.

Lili and I had also had a lot of time together to rest from the wedding and continue to cement our bond. I'd discovered what a good sounding board she was as I was thinking about suspects and motives, and I'd had the chance to see her teach a course. She was expanding her view of the future, too, thinking about more teaching and more experimentation with her computer tools.

We passed Ethan and his beagle Daisy, and I waved. "We're heading out in a little while. Nice to have met you."

"You too," he said. "That was crazy on Friday at the dog park, wasn't it? I was glad Daisy and I were near the exit and we got out fast. I spoke to the police detective and told him I happened to be looking up at the sky while Dr. M was talking, and I saw someone on the roof of the building next door."

"The shooter?"

"That's what he thinks. I couldn't say much. The person I saw was wearing long pants and a hunting jacket, but I had the impression it was a woman. I can't even say why, maybe because of her height or the way she moved."

"You didn't see her around afterward?" I asked.

Ethan shook his head. "No, the detective asked that, too. She could have been anyone from the town, even an outsider, though I think you'd have to know Centerbury to figure out you could shoot someone from that roof."

Rochester pulled forward and I said goodbye to Ethan. My big, inquisitive golden had enjoyed himself in our new surroundings, sniffing lots of new scents and making the acquaintance of new dogs, including Daisy and Janie. I wondered, not for the first time, how deep a dog's memory was. Would Rochester remember these two, and miss them?

A few months before, I'd discovered the breeder where Rochester had been born, and reunited him with his mother, and one of his littermates. He'd accepted them both readily—but was that just because they were sweet goldens? Did he have any memory of being a little blind puppy, sucking at his mother's teat?

How about the first young family who adopted him, who quickly decided he was too much for them to handle, and who'd surrendered him to the shelter, where Caroline Kelly, my next-door-neighbor, had adopted him? Did he recall Caroline, and how he had helped me and Rick figure out who killed her? That had been our first case together.

Or was he happy living in the moment, with two loving parents, a warm home, and plenty of food and treats? I looked down at him as we climbed the hill toward the inn. He was such a sweet, happy boy. If he had any difficult memories he had moved past them.

As we approached the inn, members of Dr. M's party were loading up cars and SUVs and saying goodbye. Henry Rozell was loading a long gun bag into the back of his vehicle, so I assumed that Pete had released his guns to him. Because he'd been so angry and aggressive, I wondered how long he'd stay on Dr. M's board.

Food of the Dogs

Beverly and Katherine were standing beside a taxi, their bags already in the open trunk. Heading to the airport, I guessed.

Dr. M, Winston and Zoe were clustered around a Range Rover with Wisconsin plates. He and his daughter were hugging, and I heard Winston was going to drive back to Wisconsin with his father and his sister. That was good. They were a family that needed some time to grieve and to bond.

I saw Pete Ecker walk up to them, and hoped he had some good news to share. I wanted to go over and hear what he had to say, but Rochester had other ideas. He kept tugging me toward a hedge that ran alongside the property.

The dog can be headstrong, and knowing we had a long drive ahead of us, I didn't have the energy to fight with him. We took a long, circular walk around the back of the inn, and as we rounded the corner, I realized why he'd dragged me in that direction. A woman in a lightweight hunting jacket over jeans and fur-lined Crocs crouched behind the hedge.

That was strange enough, but then I saw her raise a rifle and take aim at something. Or someone.

Rochester tugged me toward her as I called out "Hey! Put that gun down! You could hurt somebody."

She turned abruptly toward me, and I saw her dark hair. It looked like Sue Flocky from that distance, but it could have easily been her sister. She stood up, took one last look at whatever she was aiming at, and then ran down toward the creek. Very quickly she disappeared between the trees.

Rochester strained to follow her, and though I knew it was foolish, I let him run, though I kept a close hand on his leash as my feet raced to keep up with him. I heard someone running behind me but didn't want to stop and see who it was.

Rochester and I pushed our way through the trees at the creek's edge, and I stumbled on a rock and had to grab a tree trunk to keep from falling into the water. That's when I saw Pete approaching in jeans and a UVM sweatshirt under his open parka.

"A woman had a gun," I shouted back to him. Rochester circled back to me to make sure I was okay, and then took off again. Fortunately the woman we were chasing had left the screen of the trees and dashed down an alley between two houses.

We rushed up someone's lawn after her and into the alley, with Pete right behind me. By the time we reached the street, she was a block away. "I've got this," Pete said, as he ran past me. "You get back to the hotel."

Chapter 35
Champion

Rochester and I hurried up the hill to where Dr. M, Zoe and Winston still stood beside the Land Rover as a chill breeze blew down from the mountains. Janie was already in the back, and Rochester went up to sniff her.

"Was that you yelling?" Dr. M asked. "The police detective who was here talking with us took off at a run."

"It was. One of Jason Evangelos's sisters was back there, hiding behind the hedge. She had a rifle, aimed in your direction."

He sagged against the SUV. "So many people who hate me," he said. "I've only tried to do good in my life."

"You have, Daddy," Zoe said, putting her arm around him. "You've helped a lot of dogs."

He shook his head. "But the people."

"I think Athena Souris is having some kind of mental breakdown," I said. "Perhaps it was seeing you, or maybe she has let her grief for her brother take over her mind."

"I can't take responsibility for that young man's death," Dr. M said. "Veterinary medicine is hard, and you have to let your ego go and learn to take advice from others. If you don't feel qualified to perform a particular operation, you ask for help."

He looked at me. "Jason didn't. Even when I was there, he was headstrong, sure that he knew everything he needed to know. I pulled his bacon from the fire a few times, saving animals who might not otherwise have made it."

He straightened his shoulders. "I hope they find that woman and prosecute her to the full extent of the law. My son was a good man and he didn't deserve to die."

"You didn't deserve to have her try and kill you either," Winston said.

While we were talking, Pete Ecker ran up the hill, his open jacket flapping. "Did you see who it was you were chasing?" he asked me.

"I'm not sure. It could have been Sue Flocky, or it could have been her sister. I saw some photos of them online and they're about the same size. The woman who ran was wearing a watch cap so I couldn't see much of her hair, but what I did see was jet black, and both sisters have hair that color."

He pulled me aside. "Tell me exactly what you saw," he said. We walked over to the edge of the driveway and he pulled a small notebook from his pocket.

I described it in as much detail as I could, from Rochester tugging me in that direction, to seeing the rifle and yelling at the woman. Then chasing her until Pete took over.

He wrote some notes and then shook his head. "I told Dr. Mihaly to stay close to the Inn where he'd be safe. I never anticipated that one of the Evangelos sisters would come over here to ambush him."

"Whichever one it is, there's something wrong with her," I said. "She went from giving Dr. M the wrong pills to killing Alistair and then shooting at Dr. M at the dog park. That's an escalation that's very troubling. Maybe it's a mental breakdown, or just her grief taking over her rational thought. Keep in mind that you don't know which sister you're after, so be very careful."

"I will. Marilyn's husband can watch the baby this afternoon so she's going to Olives and Feta with me to talk to Sue, and maybe we'll find Athena there, too."

He shook my hand. "Thanks for everything, Steve. Have a good trip back to Pennsylvania."

"You'll let me know what you find?" I asked. "I'd like the closure."

"As much as I can tell you."

He left, and we said our goodbyes to Dr. M and his family and the staff members we'd met.

"It has been a very long and difficult week," Dr. M said. "But I'm glad we got to meet you and Lili and Rochester. Having him around helped perk up Janie, and I'm grateful for that."

"It certainly has been an interesting honeymoon," I said. "I've said it before, but I'll repeat that I'm very sorry for your loss, and I hope that you can hold onto the good memories of Alistair."

"I'm sure this will all hit me eventually," he said. "Fortunately, both Zoe and Winston are coming back to Wisconsin with me, so we'll have some time to heal as a family."

Winston got into the driver's seat of the SUV, with Dr. M behind him and Zoe in the back seat, and Winston tooted the horn as they drove away.

Ophelia came outside with a paper bag of pastries and sandwiches for our ride home. "Everything's dog friendly," she said. "So you and your best pal can share."

We thanked her and hugged her. "I'll post a great review online," Lili said. "I hope you get lots of new business and the inn is a huge success."

"We'll keep working on it." She turned to me. "I don't know if I ever properly thanked you for finding Ming Chow." She lowered her voice. "I know you didn't get much thanks from Zoe Mihaly."

"Rochester loves finding things," I said. "I'm happy to give him opportunities." She laughed and we walked out to the SUV. Lili used her phone's app to direct me out of Centerbury on the route back to the New York State Thruway.

"I can see that life with you is always going to be interesting," Lili said, as we joined traffic on a two-lane road across Vermont.

"It took the honeymoon to convince you of that?"

She laughed. "No, I already knew. When I was ready to give up photojournalism and look for a teaching job, I worried that an academic life would be boring after everything I'd been through. I welcomed that. I was tired of people shooting at me, overwhelmed by the sadness of what I'd seen around the world."

She looked out the window, and Rochester brought his head up between the seats. His long tongue lolled out.

"I'd only been at Eastern for a semester before I met you," she continued, after a moment. "I thought you were handsome and sweet and smart, but I was worried that I'd get tied down to a suburban lifestyle where one day rolled into the next, and eventually I'd wake up and realize the world had passed me by."

She turned back. "You keep me guessing, Mr. Levitan. And I like that. There's a tension to life with you that helps me balance out the ordinary world of the college with the desire for adventure that's still somewhere in my heart."

"I'm glad to hear it," I said. "I never want to hold you back, if you decide you want to take on an assignment, or even make a career change. I'm your biggest fan. I may hold Rochester on a leash, but never you."

"And you let him run often," Lili said. "Friar Lake is a great place for you because it's your own little kingdom where you have the flexibility to take off on investigations if you want. It's a place both you and your dog can run free."

To emphasize her point, Rochester leaned over and licked her cheek, and she laughed.

I looked in the rear-view mirror. "There's a Toyota sedan that has been following us since we left Centerbury," I said.

Chapter 36
An Explosive Moment

Lili gently pushed Rochester's head down and turned to look out the back window. "I can't tell who's driving," she said. "Hold on." She leaned down and pulled one of her cameras out of the bag at her feet, and attached the zoom lens to it.

"Stay down, Rochester," she said, as she turned back, this time with the camera at her eye. "Hard to get much focus with both cars moving. But it's a woman, with dark hair. And there's another woman beside her."

My heart rate accelerated. "Could it be Sue Flocky and her sister?" I asked.

"Can't tell." She faced forward again, put the camera down and picked up her phone. After tapping for a bit, she said, "There's no town of any size between here and the bridge over Lake Champlain. But there's a visitor's center on the other side of the bridge. There are bound to be people there, maybe even a state trooper. Why don't we pull in there and see if the car follows us?"

"And what if it does?" My voice was rough. "What if it is Sue Flocky and her sister, and they have a rifle, and they're angry that I chased them away from the inn this morning?"

"We can't run all the way back to Stewart's Crossing, worrying about who's behind us," she said. "We need to stop and take a stand. I learned that years ago when I was in Beirut. The reporter I was with was sure that a terrorist was following us, but we didn't have cell phones back then and there was no way to alert anyone or call for help."

I kept looking in the rear-view mirror. The Toyota was still behind us. "What did you do?"

"We didn't know where the nearest police station was, and we didn't want to lead anyone back to the hotel where we were staying. So we pulled up in front of a shopping center and parked."

"Then what?"

"The car behind us kept moving. A little girl was looking out the back window. So it probably wasn't a terrorist following us."

"I don't suppose you can see if there are any children in the car behind us."

"Didn't see one. But that doesn't mean much."

Route 125 was only two lanes wide, and there was enough traffic coming toward us that the Toyota behind us couldn't pass, even if I slowed considerably. "Do me a favor," I said. "Call Pete Ecker and ask if he's gotten hold of Sue or her sister yet."

She put the phone on speaker as it rang. "This is Pete."

"Pete, it's Steve Levitan. There's a car following us on Route 125 as we're heading home and we're worried. Have you been able to find Sue Flocky or Athena Souris?"

"I'm at the restaurant now with Aristotle Flocky. He says that Sue and Athena left about an hour ago, and he says he doesn't know where they're going."

"I don't!" I heard a man protest in the background.

"So they could be behind you," Pete said. "I've already notified the State Police to put a BOLO out on Sue's Toyota."

"That's a Toyota behind us," I said. My voice got strangled as I asked, "What color?"

"DMV records call it gray," Pete said. "Could be silver or even a dirty white."

Lili turned around to look behind us. "The car behind us looks like silver in this light."

"Where on Route 125 are you?" Pete asked.

Lili glanced at the directions on her own phone. "We just passed a street called Ten Acre Drive," she said.

"That leads to a campground. There's another one coming up on your right, but you don't want to stop there because there won't be any security. You're going to have to keep going toward the bridge. I'll see if I can get someone out Route 17. That meets up with 125 just before the bridge."

"What do we do if no one gets here in time?"

"There's a visitor's center on the New York side of the bridge. I'm going to call and make sure there's security there. If there is, you can pull in there, and we'll let New York take over the chase. I'll call you back when I hear from the visitor's center, but you might not get much cell service out there."

He ended the call and I looked at Lili. "Do what he says," she said. "Keep driving. Maybe it's not the two sisters. Or maybe they're behind us because this is the easiest way out of the state."

I took a few deep, calming breaths as I drove. Farms stretched out to the right of us, and the lake was to our left, with a screen of trees between us. Most of the deciduous trees had already lost their leaves, which gathered in piles by the roadside.

Lili looked at both our phones. "No signal," she said. "So we're on our own."

Finally we saw the bridge over Lake Champlain to our left, and it rose up like a welcome. As we approached the intersection of Route 17 I thought I spotted a flashing light to our right, but I wasn't sure. It could have been a trick of the light on the lake, or wishful thinking on my part.

We passed the cluster of small, red-roofed buildings of Chimney Point State Historic Site, one of the earliest settlements on the lake. About a dozen cars were parked there, probably belonging to a group of fishermen in cold-weather clothes with long poles and lines dangling down to the water.

Pete had told us to keep going, so we headed toward the bridge, which was built of steel trusses, with an arching center section. The bridge was only two lanes wide, so there was no place for me to pull over, and no opportunity for the car behind us to pass. I worked at keeping my breathing steady as we crossed, the placid lake water beneath us a contrast to how I felt inside.

After what seemed like a long time, but was probably only a few minutes, we crossed the bridge and spotted the Welcome to New York sign, and beyond it the entrance to the visitor's center. It was a simple, gray-shingled building.

I let out a deep sigh of relief, and signaled my turn. We pulled in, and I gripped the steering wheel, willing the Toyota behind us to keep going. But instead, it followed us into the parking lot.

"What are they doing?" I asked Lili. I made sure the car doors were locked.

The Toyota parked across from us, so we had a head-on view of it. Both women spilled out of the car. The driver got out first. A short woman in a hunting jacket and fur-lined Crocs. The other woman had a similar build, and both Lili and I recognized her as Sue Flocky.

They hurried toward us. Lili leaned forward. "I don't like the looks of this," she said.

Then, instead of heading toward us, they veered diagonally toward the visitor's center. "What the..." I said.

Rochester woofed.

"The bathroom," Lili said. "I recognize that kind of run."

"Then we should get out of here," I said.

Lili shook her head. "We'll be on the same kind of two-lane road for miles," she said. "I say we stay here and wait for them to leave. Or the police to catch up to them."

"Fine. But I'm going to pull around behind the building so they won't see the car when they leave."

I turned the engine on, and Rochester began to whimper. "Don't worry, boy, it will be all right," Lili said, stroking his head.

I couldn't park completely out of sight, but I hoped that the two women would be in a hurry to get back to their car and keep moving. Rochester wouldn't calm down, though. "I think he has to pee," I said.

"He'll have to wait," Lili said. "They won't be in there long."

Rochester's whimpering increased, and he nudged my head. "I don't think he can wait," I said. "I don't want him to have an accident in the car. We've still got a long way to drive."

I opened my door. The women were still in the visitor's center. I hoped there was only one stall so one of them had to wait for the other. I hopped out and opened the back door, and Rochester jumped to the ground eagerly and took off toward a pine tree.

He squatted, and my heart sank. This wasn't going to be a quick pee. I followed him and stood there awkwardly while he evacuated a loose stream of diarrhea. "I'm sorry, boy," I said. "You ate something that didn't agree with you, huh?"

I was so involved with thinking about him and how I was going to get him cleaned up for the ride home that I was startled to hear a car horn beep. I looked up and saw Sue Flocky and her sister approaching us.

"You're the one!" Athena said. "You screwed up my chance to finally make that lousy Dr. M pay for what he did to my brother!"

Rochester was still squatting, but he looked up at them inquisitively, his nostrils quivering.

They stopped a few feet from us. "If I can't make him pay, I'll make you," Athena said, and she pulled a gun out of her jacket pocket. It looked a lot like a Smith & Wesson, though it was hard to tell from that distance.

"Athena, no," Sue said. "We need to get moving."

"The police are going to catch me eventually," Athena said. "If I'm going to jail for one murder it might as well be for two."

Suddenly, Rochester sprang into action. There was a nasty smell in the air as he jumped past me, tackling Athena. The gun went off, the bullet hitting the pine tree with a bang. Athena fell to the ground, Rochester on top of her.

Out of the corner of my eye, I saw flashing red and blue lights, but I couldn't wait for the police to arrive. I ran over to Athena and tried to wrest the gun from her grasp.

"You! Don't even think about moving, Sue!"

I recognized Lili's voice as she came running toward us. Sue stood there, frozen, as I grabbed Athena's wrist with one hand and the gun with the other. As Rick had trained me in the past, I twisted the gun down, with Athena's finger still on the trigger. That motion broke her finger, and she screamed in pain and released her grip.

I stood up, pointing the gun down at her.

"Get this dog off me!" she cried, as she cradled her finger. Rochester sat on her stomach, keeping her immobilized.

"Vermont State Police" a voice shouted from behind me. "Everyone stand down. Sir, put the gun down."

I looked over and saw a khaki-suited trooper with his own gun pointed at me. I bent down and laid it carefully on the ground, then stepped back. "Rochester, come to me," I said. He daintily stepped away from Athena, and I noticed that her hunting jacket had fallen open to reveal a white blouse beneath it.

Which was stained with streaks of Rochester's diarrhea. Too bad for her.

A New York state trooper arrived as I began to tell my story to the Vermont cop. It took a while to spill everything out to both of them, while Athena and Sue remained silent. Then the Vermont trooper stepped away and spoke into his radio for a while.

When he returned, he turned to the New Yorker and said, "Their story checks out. I just spoke to a cop in the town they came from. And the license plate on the Toyota matches the BOLO I heard."

The Vermont cop cuffed both women and led them to his car, while the New York trooper asked for my license and registration. He scanned them and then handed them back to me. "Do you think those women were following you?"

"Hard to say," I said. "Detective Ecker from Centerbury can fill you in, but I think it's just that both of us were trying to get out of town at the same time."

"I'll let you get on your way, then."

"As soon as we get the dog cleaned up," I said. Lili stayed with him while I went into the mens room and got a batch of damp paper towels. By the time I finished, he was clean and I felt drained.

"I'll drive for a while," Lili said as we walked back to the car. "Do you think they were after us because you chased Athena earlier today?"

"I doubt it. There aren't that many ways out of Centerbury. Heading south would have kept them in Vermont for a long time. As it is, they nearly made it." I smiled. "And Athena will be wearing a reminder of Rochester for a while."

Chapter 37
Of Course

After that adventure, the long, boring stretch of Thruway was a simple run. Cars and trucks moved around us, and we went around them. I dug through the bag of Rochester's various pills and treats and found a couple of chewable tablets to settle his stomach. Then I opened the bag Ophelia had given us, and we ate and drank as we continued our way to Stewart's Crossing, though Rochester was annoyed I wouldn't give him anything to eat.

As Lili drove, Rochester dozed on the back seat and I turned and looked out the window at the trees in full color. Our leaf-peeping honeymoon had been a success in several ways. Lili and I had been drawn closer by the experience of sharing our vows, and then being on vacation together. She'd taken some great photographs and been spurred to think about her next chapter, and I'd been able to exercise my curiosity and bring some justice and comfort to a devastated family.

We were approaching Albany and the intersection with I-90, the Adirondack Northway that headed west, when Lili said, "The sign says that there's a mall at this exit. You mind if we stop for a short break? I could use the rest room and there's probably a food court."

I leaned forward. "Crossgates Mall," I said. "You know I love a good mall. Sure, let's stop."

I walked Rochester along the perimeter of the mall, next to a verdant hillside that was fenced off to protect a species of rare butterflies. Lili got us food, and we sat outside with the dog to eat. It was warmer than it had been in Centerbury, though we knew that winter would be coming soon.

"I haven't told you that I've been exchanging emails with Saul, have I?" I asked, as Rochester nibbled pieces of sliced turkey from my sandwich.

"My cousin Saul? Why?"

"I asked what else we should do in El Salvador while we're there for Talia's wedding. Should we plan to come earlier, or stay later? That kind of thing."

"Really? We haven't even finished one trip and you're already planning the next?"

"April will be here before you know it," I said. "I want to make sure this trip is extra special for you. Not just seeing your family, but having some fun and taking some photographs."

"You're sweet," she said, and squeezed my hand. We finished eating and got back on the road for another four hours.

I was still exhausted by the time we pulled into our driveway. "If I'd known I would be this tired after a vacation, I'd have extended my leave an extra day." I yawned. "We both have to go to work tomorrow."

"I kept my calendar clear for the next few days," Lili said. "You did, too, didn't you?"

"Yeah, but stuff always comes up," I said.

We unloaded the car, and I took Rochester out for a walk. "Happy to be back, boy?" I asked, as he pulled me down the street, stopping periodically to sniff out any news that had happened while we were gone. "I know I am. It's fun to travel, but like Dorothy said, there's no place like home."

The streetlamps and house lights were welcoming sights. I was back on familiar ground, and though I was exhausted, I was eager to get back to my regular life. One that was only going to be sweeter because Lili and I had formalized our relationship and celebrated it with our friends and family.

We stopped in front of Joey and Mark's house and I was sure that their golden, Brody, had left Rochester a detailed message because he took so long to sniff everywhere. We finally made it back home, and I joined Lili in bed. "Did you have fun on our honeymoon?" she asked.

"We got to spend time together, and Rochester and I solved a murder, with your help," I said. "The three of us made a great team."

"I liked the way we were both able to do our own thing, but still be together more than we can here," she said. "Between your job and mine it sometimes feels like we don't get a chance to talk much. I'd like to work on that."

"I agree. More talking." I turned to face her. "And now, more sleeping."

Rochester was already asleep on the floor beside me, his legs splayed out and his head resting on the carpet. His humans joined him for a long, well-earned sleep. Though I wasn't happy that he was up at his regular time on Monday morning, sniffing my face to alert me that he was ready for his walk.

Over breakfast, Lili and I went over our week. She had a department meeting to run, and a class to teach, and I had a couple of events scheduled at Friar Lake. "How about a date night Thursday?" I asked. "We could drive up to that French place in New Hope."

"That sounds lovely." She kissed me, and I wished for a moment we were back in Vermont and we had nothing more to do than hop back into bed together.

Instead, we pulled apart and I drove Rochester up the River Road to Friar Lake. Though I'd done my best to keep up with the flood of emails while we were away, I spent all morning and most of the afternoon at the computer, answering messages, and filling out forms.

During the summer, Eastern's faculty-run calendar committee had agreed to President Babson's request to move the start of the spring term back to February 1, and schedule an intersession for the month of January. Lili and a friend had put together a course on the cultural history of the food of the Caribbean, and we'd be hosting the beginning and ending ceremonies at Friar Lake. I had a lot of work ahead of me to pull all that together.

Rochester and I walked over to Joey's office after lunch. "How's everything going?" I asked.

As usual, the stone building smelled like machine oil with an overlay of air freshener. Rochester settled down on the floor, spreading out his four legs.

"I'm putting together a to-do list for the intersession," Joey said. "I want to check every bedroom and make sure there's nothing needed to prepare them. And I'm sure I'll keep adding to the list." He sat back in his chair. "Could have used some help from you and Rochester at home the other day, though."

I sat across from him in an old office chair that had been discarded from the campus. "For what?"

"Brody slipped out while I was letting someone in the front door. Took off like a greyhound down the street. Mark and I had to both go out and circle around before we finally corralled him near the clubhouse."

"Sorry we weren't there. Rochester had his nose to the ground in Vermont." I gave him a brief version of the clues the dog had found, starting with the little girl's stuffed dragon.

He reached down to chuck Rochester behind his long, soft ears. "You're a piece of work, aren't you, boy? At least you're better behaved than your pal Brody."

"But you love Brody just as much I as love Rochester."

"Most of the time," Joey said, with a laugh.

Rick called late in the afternoon. "Got the subpoena for the phones of the two aides who were on duty at Crossing Manor when the thefts happened," he said. "Bethanne Williams and Shenita Wright. According to the logs they have to fill out, Shenita answered the first patient's call buzzer, and Bethanne the second. A minute after Shenita logged her response, there's a brief call on her cell. She insists it was a butt dial because the call only lasted about ten seconds."

"Long enough to talk to her accomplice," I said. I was in my office, looking out the window at the trees starting to change colors. In a few days, Friar Lake would be able to rival Vermont for its display.

"You got it. The man she called is her boyfriend, and he has a drug rap a mile long. We're pulling him in for questioning this afternoon."

"Good luck," I said.

I took Rochester out for a walk around Friar Lake after that. I felt satisfied with myself. Lili and I had carried off our wedding, reception, and honeymoon. We were back home, safe and sound. I'd been able to help Rick with a case, and provided some advice to Pete Ecker as well. I really wanted to know what had happened in Centerbury after we left, but I waited for him to call me.

His call came through later that afternoon. "You might be interested to know we searched the Flocky residence and came up with two weapons," he said. "A Smith & Wesson and a Ruger AR-556 rifle. We're having ballistics tests run on both weapons but I feel pretty confident we're going to find a match to the ammunition used to kill Anthony Mihaly and wound his father."

"So it was Sue Flocky, not her sister?"

"Oh, according to Sue, it was all Athena's idea to get revenge on Dr. Mihaly. When she wasn't able to kill him at the hospital she encouraged Sue to go after him. So I'm building a case against both of them."

"Congratulations. Sounds like you did a good job."

"I appreciate your help, and your confidence in me when I didn't believe in myself. I'm going to push to stay as a detective when Marilyn comes back from leave. I still have a lot to learn, but I know I can do it."

"Good for you."

As I was packing up to leave, another call came through on my cell, from an unfamiliar area code and number. I was tempted to let it go to voice mail, but my curious nature overrode that idea.

"Is this Steve?" a man's voice asked.

"Who's this?"

"It's Dr. M. Detective Ecker told me they've caught the woman who shot my son." His voice broke, but he continued. "It's that nurse, Athena. He said you helped the police subdue her, and I wanted to thank you."

"I was really protecting myself and Rochester," I said. "We ran into Athena and Sue at a rest stop near the bridge over Lake Champlain and she pulled a gun on us. But I'm glad the police caught her. I hope that will bring you a measure of comfort."

"It still hurts to know she mistook Alistair for me," he said. "If I could have taken the bullet for him, I would have."

In the background I heard Zoe's voice. "Daddy. Winston and I are here for you. Can you give me the phone, please?"

He sucked back his tears. "Thank you, from the bottom of my heart."

I heard some rustling, and then Zoe said, "We'd love to send you some bags of Dr. M's Healthy Food for Rochester. Can you text your address to Daddy's number?"

"I'll do that," I said. "You guys take care."

Rochester and I went out to the car, and as usual, he jumped in through my door and climbed over to the passenger seat. "You did very well this week," I said to him. "I worried you wouldn't be able to find any clues in such a different area, but you came up as a champion."

He looked at me, his mouth wide in a doggy grin, as if to say, "Of course."

Acknowledgments

Thank you to the Bread Loaf Writer's Conference, for the opportunity to attend what has been called "summer camp for writers" and for the chance to spend time in Middlebury. That charming town is the inspiration for Centerbury, but none of the actions in this book occurred there, nor should there be an implicit attack on veterinarians here. Sam, Brody and Griffin have been helped by many wonderful vets in the past. (Though there was one nasty woman who made me cry because she wanted to neuter Sam against our wishes, and she enumerated how painful testicular cancer could be. She'll show up in a book someday!)

Once again, my beta readers helped me find errors in the manuscript. The careful attention that Andy Jackson, Bob Ronai, Jim Bessey, Judith Levitsky, Robert Kman, and Tim Brehme paid to their reading is much appreciated. Any that remain are solely my fault.

My regular calls with Joanna Campbell Slan keep me on track and help me work through knotty situations, as do my lunches with Greg Lindeblom. Zita Goldfinger DVM and Jay Luger DVM both provide excellent advice on dog-related issues. Randall Klein is a terrific editor, and I love how Kelly Nichols brings my covers to life. Special shout out to Eileen Matluck, Lynne Duvivier and Mary Ellen O'Shea for their friendship and support as well as the members of the Florida chapter of Mystery Writers of America, and the many wonderful authors I have met through my membership with that organization.

I appreciate all the emails I get from fans who have enjoyed the series, and I love hearing about your dogs. If you've enjoyed this book, or others in the series, I hope you will take a moment to post a review wherever you get your books. These really do help new readers decide if my work is something they'd like.

I miss certain elements of my college career, like the camaraderie of colleagues and the personal interaction with students, so I am grateful for the friendship of Andrea Apa and Lourdes Rodriguez-Florido. Thank you to all the writers' groups that have hired me to do Zoom presentations. I get to teach but don't have to grade papers! If you belong to a book group or writer's group that would like me to talk about my books or elements of craft, let me know via the contact link on my website, www.mahubooks.com.

Also visit the site to sign up for my newsletter and hear about new releases and appearances. I hope to be adding some goodies there soon, including deleted scenes and epilogues.

Marc, Brody and Griffin make my life sublime.

Author's Note: Easter Eggs

I can't resist dropping in Easter eggs in books, from my own experiences with my dogs to bits of my personal history. I graduated from Columbia Business School with my MBA in real estate and operations management in May, 1983, and it was hard to find a job. My finance major classmates were headed off to Wall Street, and those who'd majored in marketing were joining consumer goods companies and advertising agencies. The other real estate majors had double-majored in accounting or finance, so they were able to snag corporate jobs.

Though I went on a bunch of interviews, nothing was coming through. Then I got a call from the Pyramid Companies, based in Syracuse. They were looking for a junior construction manager; would I like to interview?

I sure would.

They flew me to their corporate headquarters in Syracuse one morning, where I had a whirlwind of interviews, and then in the afternoon I flew to Albany, where Crossgates Mall was already under construction. It was a hot, dusty afternoon as I was driven to the trailer where the team worked. I'd worn my best interview suit, which wasn't great for trudging around the site, but I was excited.

I had already graduated, and only had one serious opportunity so far. I'd met with a representative from Continental Illinois National Bank at a midtown hotel and talked about a real estate lending position with them in their Chicago office. The rep had liked me enough to bring me to Chicago for a day of interviews.

Sadly at the end of the day an HR rep told me that while they loved me, I didn't have enough accounting background to join their training program.

So I was excited to see the mall under construction, and think that I could be a part of it. I remember vividly I'd decided to put some blond dye in my hair for the summer, and I was naked, waiting to wash the dye out, when the call came through with my job offer.

I accepted, of course. Even though I wasn't thrilled about moving to Albany, or starting work at six in the morning, I wanted a job in my field.

Only later did I learn that both companies had been desperate to hire someone. Continental Illinois had been through scandals and no graduate from a good school wanted to work there, which made me feel doubly bad that even though they were desperate, they wouldn't hire me. And Pyramid had interviewed all twelve real estate majors in my class, made each one a job offer, and been rejected eleven times.

I was apparently too good at blowing my own horn in my interviews, and I quickly learned that I didn't know half of what I said I did. I heard later that they wanted to fire me after the first week, but it would have been too embarrassing to the partner who hired me, and they did actually need a warm body in that job.

Which is a long way of saying that I was happy to have Steve and Lili stop at Crossgates Mall on their way home. And that wall around the butterfly hill? That was one of my projects. Reviewing the plans, hiring the contractor and supervising the build. It wasn't much but it did give me a lot of satisfaction, and the experience at Pyramid led me to a rewarding career in shopping center construction. (You can read more about that in my comic novel, *Steve and the Blatnicks*, which draws on a lot of my background while being in my opinion, very funny.)